DIAMOND

# FLAWED DIAMOND

**Beautiful Things Can Have Hidden Flaws**

# PROLOGUE

He couldn't see much, if anything, but by all the gods he could feel – and it wasn't pleasant. His head felt like an anvil someone was testing their strength on, an unwanted mix of dull pain, sharp needles and a constant roaring. The rest of his body felt little better. There was some significant pain in his right shoulder and there was every indication of a couple of bruised or cracked ribs. It didn't help that he also felt like being rolled around in a washing machine and every movement hurt like heck. He realized that he could smell and that was about as bad as everything else: a nauseous mix of damp air, oil and urine.

Slowly Commander Andrew Martyn eased himself into consciousness. About the only thing clear to his dulled mind was that he was in some sort of boat and, by the sound of swishing water, fairly low down, maybe in the bilge. An urge to sit up resulted in failure. He remained prone, sweating profusely, but bent his head forward and looked down his battered body in the dim light available. He was dressed in a rather smart set of slacks and open-neck shirt – or at least they possibly used to look like that. Now they were more in the nature of old rags, stained and torn. He lay back and tried to force his mind out of its black pit to remember who, what and where he might be.

Scattered thoughts started to assemble themselves but lacked any coherent timeline. A picture of Angela came to mind, together with something important she had to do. God let me think he mentally shouted. A hotel lobby, a receptionist handing him a phone, a taxi, blackness. Rabaul! A glimmer of sense at last: he was, or used to be, in Rabaul, New Britain. He reached up to rub his temples hoping to clear his mind and realized that his hands were tied together. He stared vacantly at his hands, as much as he could see of them, and felt an overwhelming sense of both failure and tiredness. He slept.

Noise! Blinding light! Movement! 'Here, drink this' said a rough gravelly voice – Maori? Islander? 'Use both hands' said the voice, and a plastic bottle was pushed towards his face. He hadn't realized how thirsty he was until he had finished half the bottle of plain, cool water. By now the voice was muttering near his legs and, as one leg was pulled forcefully sideways, he felt a sharp jab into his thigh. Ouch! He slept.

# CHAPTER 1

The sleek grey warship made hardly a ripple as it nudged itself towards the pier in Melbourne. She was the light frigate 'Succeed', temporary home and workplace to some hundred or so sailors. All of them were looking forward to some shore leave when they finally reached their Sydney destination after six months operating in the Persian Gulf. That was equally the case for the skipper, Commander Peter Martyn.

Pete let out a long sigh as he settled into an armchair – there was always a degree of relief at getting alongside after a long stint at sea, just as it was often a relief to get underway again after any significant time alongside. The XO, Pete's deputy, stuck his head around the cabin door.

'All secured boss. The mail has arrived, fuel is on its way and all is well in the world.'

'Good stuff David, want a coffee? I have news.'

'Sure' responded Dave as he wandered into the relative confines of the captain's cabin and plonked himself into the spare armchair.

Pete pressed his buzzer for the steward and gave his Number 2 an appraising glance. The two officers shared a relaxed camaraderie. They worked well together and actually liked each other: indeed, there were few onboard who didn't like their skipper: he was one of nature's gentlemen. Whatever Pete was about to say was interrupted by a flustered Petty Officer steward stepping into the cabin with a muttered 'yes sir, how can I help?' He was red-faced and clearly out of breath.

Pete and the XO gave each other a bemused glance. 'Could we get a couple of coffees please PO, but maybe you could explain why you are here yourself. Are we a bit short-staffed down there or something?'

'We do have a bit of an issue in the Wardroom Sir, but I'm sure it will be sorted shortly.'

Pete smiled reassuringly but demanded 'come on PO what's going on?'

'Well', the PO started nervously, 'the new steward seems to have gone 'troppo' and he's got the others bailed up in the pantry yelling and screaming at them'.

The XO stood and said 'I'll come'. Both XO and PO steward headed off to investigate.

Pete mentally shrugged, thinking he obviously was not going to get a coffee for a while. There were worse disasters. He went for a walk around the upper deck. By the time he returned 10 minutes later there was a trio comprising the XO, Coxswain and a steward with a very hang-dog air waiting outside his cabin. Once inside he put on his serious face and looked expectantly toward the XO who had tentatively put his head around the door.

'Sir, there has been a minor altercation between stewards in the wardroom. I have the main offender outside but rather than formal defaulters I thought it might be best if you speak with him'.

'Why?' was Pete's simple rejoinder.

'He's Jewish Sir'.

'OK Dave, what's that got to do with anything?'

'Well it seems the other stewards, who had discovered that he was Jewish, started waving bacon in his face whilst preparing breakfast and he took umbrage'.

'Ah, I see' muttered Pete and, after a short pause, 'was anyone hurt?'

'No Sir'.

'Alright, have the Coxswain wheel him in'.

Within moments the steward was standing stiffly to attention in front of his captain with cap in hand and a highly nervous expression on his face.

'Steward Goldman to see the captain' barked the Coxswain, also stiffly at attention and looking decidedly menacing next to the much smaller steward.

'Explain yourself' was Pete's simple demand, looking Goldman directly in the eye to detect any sign of evasion.

'I'm sorry Sir, I got angry and lost control. It won't happen again Sir'.

Pete remained silent for a full minute, partly to let the young man stew and partly to think through his options.

'I understand there may have been some provocation' he finally said, then, more firmly, 'but that is no excuse for violent or threatening behaviour Goldman, and if the Coxswain here was to have you formally charged the consequences could be severe. You understand that?'

'Yes Sir' responded the steward somewhat meekly.

'Wait outside' ordered Pete as he gestured to the XO and Coxswain to move further into the cabin and close the door.

After a short consultation it was decided that Goldman would be directed to formally apologize to the other stewards and then take on the role of personal steward to the captain where he could be kept an eye on and also lose some leave in the process. Little did Pete know that this decision would reap some unexpected benefits at a later date. He called Dave back as he made to leave.

'My news, Dave', he began, waving a copy of the morning's signal from HQ. 'Not good, I'm afraid. We are going to be a day late getting home.'

'The troops aren't going to be too happy about that', Dave commented.

'Oh, it gets worse, Fleet', by which Pete meant the staff of their Sydney headquarters, 'seem to think we've been on a holiday cruise. We have to demonstrate that the defects in the weapon system have been fixed. They've laid on a gunnery shoot on the way back. Worse still, the Admiral is coming aboard to watch. On top of that they want a full ceremonial entry into Sydney'.

Dave winced as he was handed the signal concerned. 'I'll let everyone know', was all he said with unaccustomed prudence.

Which reminded Pete he needed to do some informing of his own and picked up his mobile. 'Hello darling, it's Pete, how are my three lovely girls?

'The younger ones are fine and far too energetic', Marie Martyn declared, 'the older one is frazzled trying to keep good order and Naval discipline. All three looking forward to seeing you my love'.

'That's why I'm calling darling, I'm afraid we are going to be a day late into Sydney. Need to get some pesky trials done first'.

After a few more shared confidences that implied a thoroughly warm welcome whenever they were back together again, the pair said their farewells.

A day later 'Succeed' was again at sea and heading up the coast toward Sydney under a slate-grey sky that was a matching backdrop for the apparently silent warship. The flecks of scattered whitecaps disguised any bow wave the vessel might have been making and it seemed to be just sitting patiently among the waves, cold and watchful. The scene was somewhat warmer inside though, and definitely watchful!

'10,000 yards, Sir, still closing: permission to engage?'

Pete could feel his body go even tenser than it had already been for the last few hours. His momentary pause was all of a few seconds but seemed like an eon and he could almost feel the glances cast in his direction from all corners of the darkened operations room.

'Clear to engage' he said, his voice crisp and businesslike.

All around, the glowing lights of radar consoles and display screens continued unaltered but the voices of the operators took on a new edge and a subtle but very real shift occurred in the focus of activity. The sense of concentration was palpable; anonymous buttons clicked, clipped orders were transmitted into microphones, distant bells sounded their warning.

'Kerumph'. The operations room shook as the forward gun, only slightly muted by distance and three steel bulkheads, roared into life. The after gun, smaller, more distant and muffled, joined in and there followed sixty seconds of almost constant bedlam as voices, radio speakers, buzzers and machinery competed with the 'crump' of gunfire - each shot sending violent tremors through the ship. Pete's body screamed for some sort of physical action. He glanced around the room, his eyes well accustomed to the gloom, noted the still orderly arrays of screens and hunched operators and forced himself to concentrate on the closing radar blip.

'Lost target, Lost target, cease firing!' came a disembowelled voice over the central speaker. Pete's attention remained firmly glued to the phosphor screen to his front. Clutter, sea return and over twenty numbered blips seemed to fill the display but it was just one track that commanded his attention. One track in just a few square centimetres of empty screen: one all-important blip that brought a slow smile of relief to his face - because it wasn't there! Pete realised suddenly that he had been unconsciously holding his breath and relaxed his lungs with an audible sigh. As if this were a formal cue, other operators throughout the darkened room leaned back from their illuminated panels; a few wry smiles were exchanged. Even the impersonal hum of densely-packed electronics seemed to take on a slightly more relaxed note.

'Well done everyone', said Pete evenly, trying to keep an overwhelming sense of relief out of his voice. 'I'm going up top'.

One door and a short length of passageway later and Peter Martyn was in a different world. He had subconsciously forgotten it was day-time and a well-timed burst of sunlight as he stepped onto the Bridge caught him slightly by surprise. The Bridge team were all going about their business in that quiet but professional manner that reflected the age-old formality of the Service. And so they should, thought Pete, especially now with 'The Glove' watching every move. As if in response to that thought 'The Glove', in the form of Rear Admiral Patrick Usher, Australia's Maritime Commander, who also happened to be Pete's uncle, made his presence obvious.

'I think a cup of coffee might be in order, Peter', his strong but mellow voice drifted gently across from the Captain's chair (my chair thought Pete with a twinge of irritation, surprising himself with his proprietorial feeling). 'I'm sure your team are up to a bit of salvage by themselves, so why don't we go below?' It wasn't a question, of course, and Pete merely shot a look across at the Officer of the Watch to make sure he had heard before turning to lead the way to his cabin.

It is an amazing knack of sailors the world over to affix enduring and remarkably perceptive nick-names to the personalities they encounter. Probably no-one remembered from whom or when the Admiral had acquired his, but there was little doubting its aptness. Of basic Irish stock two or three generations ago, he had all the toughness of that ilk, all the charm and smoothness, yet absolutely none of the fiery temper. His reprimands, when delivered, had all the attributes of cold steel and the effect of a knockout blow. His manner, though, would remain calm and constant with no-one ever able to recall him showing his feelings in public. 'The Glove', thought Pete, was worth emulating and was living up to his name right now, having been embarked by helicopter some hours previously. 'Succeed', one of the most capable pieces of weaponry in the Admiral's armoury, looked to be finally off the hook after reporting a faulty weapon system a month previously.

Comfortably seated in Pete's small but pleasantly furnished and very functional day cabin, the Admiral sipped Goldman's carefully prepared coffee appreciatively, eased his shoulders back into the armchair and gave his nephew a long appraising look.

'I suppose your feeling pleased with yourself'.

'More a case of relief Sir, pleased for the ship though. The guys have been putting in an awful lot of extra hours on the way back to get the systems right and it's been a pretty frustrating time for everyone. I think the crew would really appreciate it if you could see your way clear to saying a few words before you head back.'

'Mmmh...', the Admiral looked distracted, 'yes of course, that's not a problem. I'm afraid it's not them I came to speak to though, it was you: and regardless of the other day's signal, I didn't fly out here simply to witness your weapon trials. We have bigger fish to fry, you and I, and it really can't be put off any longer. The bottom-line Peter, is that I need you in New Guinea - or more accurately I think your brother does.'

It had been a long day and realization was a little slow to dawn in Pete's eyes. As it did the soft grey turned to steel and the eye-lids perceptibly closed. None of this was lost on the Admiral: he certainly had all the attention he had wanted!

'We seem to have a problem in Port Moresby. I'm well aware that you're not on the best of terms with your brother. What you may not know', he continued without needing any confirm-ation, 'is that Andrew was promoted and given that appoint-ment on my personal recommendation. Well for some months now it would appear that things - by which I mean your brother, his work and my credibility - have been turning to custard. I want someone I can trust up there to find out what the hell's going on, and by someone, I mean you.'

Pete's face, until then grim and frozen, cracked just enough to allow speech. 'But Sir as matters stand the ship is earmarked for northern deployment straight after leave and the XO is due for replacement. Anyway', he continued more cautiously, 'Andrew and I are the same rank now. It wouldn't be proper for me to in-vestigate him - especially as we're related'.

'Minor details, Peter' the Admiral rose quietly to his feet. 'Look, I understand your sensitivities and am not looking for an answer right now but I will make my position clear - which is more than I can say for the scene in Moresby. I've made plenty of errors in my time but misjudging your brother wasn't one of them. I believe he's a good officer, whatever your personal opin-ion. Matters seem to be getting out of control, though, and now he seems to have gone missing. What's worse is that he is now a key suspect in a murder enquiry. The picture the High Commis-sioner paints is not a pretty one and it doesn't make sense: not to me. Peter, you're my pick to sort this out quietly and effectively and I would like you up there. If it's the ship you're worried about, don't! David Bell is a good Executive Officer, he's already up for promotion and he'll make a damn fine CO - you said so yourself. Anyway, think on what I've said. There is a file here I would like you to read before Friday when you get into Sydney; we can discuss what needs to be done following that. Meanwhile, I want to walk around your ship, after which I'll have a word with the troops so you can kindly organize the chopper to take me off in an hour.'

Pete stood and maintained stunned silence as he followed the Admiral out of the cabin. He hadn't exactly stormed out, but his manner was unusually brusque and he was clearly in no mood to brook further argument. Pete muffled a long sigh and a guarded 'Oh shit!'.

The next hour or so passed in something of a blur. The target drone wasn't worth salvaging, but recovering what bits remained at least kept Pete's 'green' conscience quiet and denied the local fishermen an excuse to claim for supposedly damaged nets. 'The Glove' had been effusive in his praise of the ship and her crew and, after handshakes and smiles all round, was on his way back to Sydney courtesy of the ship's embarked helicopter. As the relative calm of evening routine settled upon the ship, Pete sent for Goldman.

'Set another place at table please, Goldman, and ask the Executive Officer to join me for dinner; say about 1930 after he's finished rounds.'

Steward Goldman nodded and left thinking something was clearly afoot. In Navy destroyers the captain traditionally ate on his own, whilst the Executive Officer presided at the Wardroom table where the remainder of the officers ate. Two and two quickly made five and the XO was almost the last to hear any of the myriad of rumours then abounding.

'Come in Dave, how about a drink?'

Dave entered the captain's cabin shaking his head and smiling before noticing that Pete was already proffering a glass of wine. 'Good grief, you're serious - what's the occasion?' He couldn't quite keep the surprise out of his voice, for even impressing the Maritime Commander and getting the nod for operational deployment again was hardly reason to break the unwritten rule that officers didn't drink at sea. Hardly reason for Commander Peter Martyn anyway!

'Not obligatory Dave, just the one, and you might just feel the occasion suits as I think we could be celebrating something: I'm just not sure what!'

David Bell didn't actually drop his wine glass, but he was patently suffering the immediate onset of both intrigue and anticipation. The little grey cells of his perceptive mind were clearly running around in different directions. Slowly he sat. Subconsciously, glass went to mouth and he sipped slowly. 'OK, I'm intrigued', he acknowledged.

His CO lifted one hand, palm forward, and with the other reached over to a slim folder of papers he had evidently been reading.

'Let's eat and all shall be revealed!' said a smiling but somewhat rueful Pete.

# CHAPTER 2

Ivor Slavinski was not a nice person. He was settled comfortably but sleepily in an airline seat that displayed little room for free movement. Ivor was a large man in every sense of the term. 'Two metres up and two axe-handles across' was a reasonable description and one of which his colleagues were fond. His overall build evoked strength and only the closest inspection of this patently fit man would reveal those minor marks of dissolution often associated with frequent indulgence in life's many pleasures. Nothing too obvious: the slightly sallow cheeks of the smoker; faint but broken veins about eyes and nose; a hint of slackness in the stomach. A big man with big appetites! He was in the process of demonstrating the latter now.

'Top her up Darl, there's a good girl' he said, continuing the aerial wave of the wine glass he had used to gain the attention of the hostess. 'That's the Shiraz', he added with total superfluity.

The hostess gave a tight but polite smile. 'Certainly, sir'. She spoke softly and turned toward the galley knowing full well his gaze would be locked on to her legs. No harm there, she thought, he had been checking out all the hostesses' attributes ever since boarding in Cairns some two hours ago. Lord, though, she hated being called 'Darl' and was especially irritated because of her initial attraction to this particular passenger. Even camouflaged in an expensive suit, his muscular physique had been hard to miss when he took his second row Business Class seat and his smile was bright and easy. Fortyish, she thought, seemingly well-to-do and outwardly charming in a rough and ready sort of way. There was something she had seen in his eyes though, a dull emptiness that evoked a kind of emotional vacuum and a certainty that any relationship with this man would be decidedly one-sided. Equally, his eating habits were appalling.

Ivor had already noticed that he had been subtly appraised. It had warranted a mild and passing fillip to his ego then simple acceptance. He simply couldn't give a damn about what this girl thought of him, or any other for that matter – there were plenty of pretty girls in this world and he had access to more than his fair share. It didn't stop him looking at a good pair of legs, though, just another of life's simple pleasures in an otherwise complicated world!

His life had been devoid of many of life's pleasures until relatively recently. Survival was about the most he had ever hoped for in his early days in post-war London. His father an escapee from a Polish slum; abandoned by parents who were too stupid to deny Judaism and got themselves shot for their stubbornness. At least they had managed to shove his father into the back corner of a dingy cellar before they went to their martyrdom. In retrospect it was a matter of some surprise to his father that he had survived. Scrounging, stealing, begging, but always cold, hungry and tired was the ancestral tale and he had rarely let a week pass by without regaling Ivor with the horrors of what passed for his childhood, and which had simply ended with the end of the adults' war. At that time, he had managed to slink aboard a dirty tramp steamer in Gdansk that promptly sailed into an even greater Hell. Alternately thrown about like a ragdoll and slopping around in a foot of water in the dark, with an awareness of an empty stomach that seemed determined to become even emptier. Unconsciousness was probably blessed relief, he recalled, because it had been nearly three days later when he had been found, dried, fed and thrown back onto the streets in a place called London.

Ivor did not believe in God – the one of his Jewish ancestors or any other. If there was a God at all, he mused, it was the one who gave him the courage to go to sea ten years previously after his long-suffering parents had died. Actually, it had not just been courage. He had embraced God for a while. Street-wise

and mature but still poor at twenty-eight after a seemingly endless series of 'nowhere' jobs helping ungrateful employers move
up in the world, he noticed what seemed to him a dispropor-
tionate number of those already 'up in the world' attended the
local synagogue. Not one to miss investigating his options, Ivor
rediscovered Judaism and after a few devout attendances found
himself working for reasonable pay for a local jeweller. He was
considered promising, with a good eye for facets and flaws, and
was rapidly becoming something of an identity in the local diamond world. It was not really his fault the jeweller had a randy
fifteen-year-old daughter and his own nocturnal visits had simply been a satisfaction of mutual desires. Nonetheless, discovery brought the collective wrath of employer, temple and the
metropolitan police to his door and he really had to leave.

They were right, though, about their God working in mysterious ways, he mused, for without that little catalyst he would
not have found his ultimate haven in the Cook Islands. It had
been a tortuous path and after signing on as deck hand on the
first available steamer leaving England, he had discovered first-
hand the debilitating power of the sea on both mind and body.

He awoke to gentle shaking.

'Seat belt please sir, we will be landing shortly'.

Sure enough, QANTAS Flight 590 from Port Moresby via Cairns
made its gentle descent into Sydney and landed safely at 1pm.
Without overtly hurrying, Ivor made his way past the few trav-
ellers ahead of him and smiled broadly at the Immigration officer.

'Good to be back', he said promptly, 'Pity it's just for a couple of
days though, just a quick business meeting'.

If he thought it odd for a well-dressed Caucasian to be a citi-
zen of the Cook Islands, the custodian of Australia's border gave
no indication. The well-worn passport and accompanying visa
were in order, the name was on no 'Watch list' and so with a curt
nod, a bland smile and 'Welcome to Sydney' Ivor was on his way
to Customs. Lugging a heavy attaché case but with no delaying
hold baggage, a confident Ivor was through the 'Nothing to De-

clare' exit and into Sydney's June sunshine by 1.30pm. Within 30 seconds he was drawing luxuriously on his first cigarette for over six hours and enjoying a double hit of nicotine on top of the patch he was wearing on his left shoulder.

Temporarily sated, Ivor impatiently joined the taxi queue whilst jabbing numbers one-handed into his rather sleek cellphone.

'Thomas, its Ivor – you have my order ready?'

'OK, I will be there in 20 minutes'

The queue for cabs was now filling up rapidly from behind and thinning somewhat less quickly in front, but Ivor was sliding quietly into the back seat of his allotted cab, replete with gaudy Hindi mini-shrine and Kashmiri driver, before he had a chance to light up another Dunhill.

'Sylvania please m'boy, Box Road' he barked, focussed on removing the airline tags from his attaché case and stuffing them in his pocket. He checked his slim gold Seiko and relaxed: plenty of time.

'What number?' queried the driver, 'You know the place?'

'Doesn't matter' responded Ivor casually, 'I'll let you know where when we get closer'.

And closer they did get, despite the maniacal airport traffic, for Sylvania is but a few kilometres from Mascot airport and the driver wanted to get rid of this low fare and return for better pickings.

'Here' snapped Ivor, 'next corner, just drop me off at that bus stop'.

Fare paid and door slammed, Ivor walked briskly back in the direction they had come until the cab had become enmeshed again in traffic then he reversed course to the nearest roadside litter bin. The entire contents of his attaché case – meaningless junk and carefully anonymous – went into the bin. Pausing to compose himself, Ivor sauntered on for a few hundred metres then, with barely a glance at the sign, ducked into a rather seedy looking electronics shop. The shop had doubtless seen better days, but they must have been a long time ago because the shop looked precisely as it had when Ivor had called on its equally seedy owner twelve months previously. The scrawled 'Closed for Lunch' sign stuck to the door with silver duct tape, and which he ignored, was about the only noticeable change.

'Hi Thomas' he called cheerily to a harassed and decidedly nervous-looking individual standing behind the littered counter, 'remember me?'.

'Course I do' responded the nervous individual, simultaneously revealing his inner London origins, 'got ya parcel right 'ere'.

Ivor leaned quickly across the counter and with one oversized hand bunched up Thomas' shirt-front and pulled him half way across the counter. He was no longer smiling.

'No, you don't remember me you stupid arsehole' spat Ivor 'the next time you remember me – and I mean to anyone' he emphasised, 'you're dead meat. Got it?'

Thomas was nodding furiously even as he was pushed backwards, sending bits and pieces of electronic wizardry and miscellaneous invoices flying in all directions. He had almost a minute then to collect himself whilst Ivor brushed down his rather travel weary and now slightly dusty suit front. He used that time to duck behind the counter and reappear clutching what looked like a small Fedex box wrapped in more of the ubiquitous silver duct tape. He took care to keep a safe distance from the counter.

'There's the small matter of five thousand then' he challenged.

Ivor reached into his breast pocket and extracted a plain but bulging envelope and slapped it down in front of him.

'That complete?' he nodded at the box in Thomas' hands.

'All to spec guv' said Thomas who seemed to regain his confidence as he passed over the box whilst reaching forward to pick up the envelope, immediately retreating to what he imagined could be a safe distance. Holding the envelope in one hand whilst tearing it open with the other, he was too busy counting to notice that Ivor had already left.

Having put a good distance between himself and the electronics shop, Ivor checked his watch for the third time whilst watching for a passing cab. 'Damn' he muttered, realising that he was showing signs of nervousness, and immediately took three or four deep slow breaths. He was no newcomer to this sort of business, but he didn't really get any pleasure from it and was never sure whether the nerves were a product of excitement, fear or just impending action. 'Stay professional' he told himself and felt rewarded as an empty cab swerved into the kerb in front of him. Thirty minutes and two cab-rides later he was ostensibly studying the offerings in the window of a neat brick real estate office in suburban Little Bay. He needed to regain his bearings. Studying maps and memorising routes never did translate into comfortable directions on the ground for him. Nonetheless, his street-wise memory served him well and within another five minutes he was standing in front of a freshly painted weatherboard house in a quiet tree-lined suburban street. Number 6 he confirmed to himself as he mentally rehearsed his lines.

'Mmh' he mouthed absently, 'too easy - looks like there's no-one home'.

He strolled up to the house with a purposeful stride in case any neighbours were looking his way and casually checked the mailbox on his way up the drive. Empty! He moved quickly through the side gate and onto the rear porch where he opened his attaché case and tore apart the binding on his newly acquired box. On went a pair of disposable surgical gloves and following that from the box came a small bunch of lock-picks. They proved unnecessary as the back door was unlocked, so through he went and immediately set about a thoroughly workmanlike search of the house. 'Workmanlike' if you were a messy worker that is, for everywhere he searched he left a trail of discarded and often broken items. After an hour of intense concentration he was sweating heavily and the house was a mess. He was searching for one simple Registered Mail envelope and had patently drawn a blank. He stood absolutely still for a minute checking for unwanted noises then strode briskly out the back door and across to a garden shed. 'Tut tut' he thought, 'very careless', and extracted a half-full tin of mower fuel from the unlocked shed. After rechecking the shaped charge and its wire trigger, he had earlier attached to the jamb of the front door he turned on the taps of the very convenient gas cooker and quickly but carefully spread the two-stroke fuel around the hallway and kitchen.

He then left the way he had come, satisfied that he had fulfilled his first mission. Within the hour he was wandering around department stores selecting random items of interest whilst taking care to limit each credit card purchase to less than the $200 limit which would call for a PIN number. Second mission accomplished! Within minutes he was settling into a private CBD apartment, having rewarded himself by booking a slim dark-haired Filipino girl from 'Independent Escorts'.

# CHAPTER 3

Marie Martyn was happy with her life. Not overtly glamorous, she was nonetheless an attractive woman. Not quite 35, she had recovered her trim figure quickly after childbirth and toned up regularly at the local gym. Benefiting from the genes of her Italian parentage, she had the mild and dusky complexion of Latin women the world over, complemented by sleek and lustrous black hair, cut severely to contemporary fashion, and the deep almond eyes of a breathing Mona Lisa. Right now, two of the three main joys of her life – twins Samantha and Rebecca – were clearly champing at the bit and trying to distract her from a leisurely coffee with friend Audrey. Audrey was her soul-mate, albeit a somewhat wealthier one, a fellow gym club member and also parent of a four-year-old at the local pre-school. Thursdays marked their weekly escape to relax and gossip over coffee and cake. That habit had begun when the children were babes in arms and from when a need for mutual support between similarly sleep-deprived mothers had been so much more necessary.

'I think you have some petitioners' murmured Audrey whilst nodding beyond Marie's left shoulder towards the girls. 'Which reminds me' she added over the cold dregs of her cappuccino, 'are you supporting truancy or have I missed something?'

'Oh, it's their pre-school day right enough' responded Marie lightly, but with an extravagant rolling of the eyes added 'blame the bloody Navy, Pete was due back this afternoon and we were all going down to the ship to meet him but they've apparently been delayed doing some test or other so now he won't be back until tomorrow. I had already arranged to pick the girls up at lunchtime so I am stuck with them for the afternoon. I hope they're not being too annoying.'

Without waiting for a response, Marie turned to an increasingly insistent Samantha who had been tugging at her sleeve for some minutes.

'Don't do that Sam, Mummy's talking' she said, though not unkindly, 'what is it?'

'We didn't get Fred's stuff' came the response in as an accusatory tone as the four-year-old could manage.

'Yes, and he's completely out of carrots' shot a pouting Rebecca in support.

'Don't worry, we'll go to the greengrocers but we need to go to the Post Office first to pick up this undelivered parcel' answered Marie, vaguely waving a small mail notification card 'now sit back down both of you and learn to be patient'.

Turning to Audrey she clarified 'Fred's the rabbit'.

'Well, I didn't really think you had taken in a lodger' noted Audrey with a twinkling eye, 'although with the amount of time Peter spends away at sea, I wouldn't really blame you. And for no good reason that reminds me its past three o' clock so I'd better get moving and pick up my own little bundle of happiness'.

Amidst much scraping of chairs and re-orientation of shopping trolleys, the two friends said their respective goodbyes and Marie headed towards the Post Office with twins impatiently in the lead.

In reflective mood, Marie absently mused about the concept of having a boarder 'with benefits'. In some ways Peter had often been like that she thought, focussed on his work and disappearing to sea for months on end. Mostly he came home dog-tired and she could hardly remember the last time they had made passionate love. It hadn't always been like that: maybe she should think about going back to work herself, even though they didn't really need the money.

Marie had been a nurse – still was she supposed. That's how she had met Pete. Hospitals and ships don't have a lot in common but they are usually crammed with young singles of the opposite sex so the occasional gravitational pull does arise. It had been a ship's party and Pete just one of a number of dashing looking officers acting as hosts. He had something of a restrained air about him, though, that set him slightly apart from the others and somehow she had ended up dancing with him and chatting the night away. He was the perfect gentleman on their subsequent dates at various Sydney restaurants. It was she who had finally felt the need to invite him to stay the night at her tiny apartment near the hospital. What a night that turned out to be! The seemingly shy – almost diffident – Peter revealed a passionate nature and stamina that fully complemented his good looks and physique. They made love all night plus most of the next day and promptly decided to live together. She well knew that he was on the rebound from some earlier relationship, but so was she, so what did that really matter?

There had been no regrets, and when the full scope of their differences and similarities became apparent it was clear that they complemented each other so well that marriage became inevitable. She was from a large migrant Italian family – some would say enormous by most standards – with a brace of brothers, two younger sisters, innumerable aunts, uncles, nieces, nephews and the whole panoply of a southern European dynasty. He was virtually alone. His parents had been killed in a car crash some years previously and he had no other family except his estranged brother and an uncle who happened to be his Admiral. But she had also been alone, having moved from the family empire in Melbourne to pursue a doomed affair with a Sydney lawyer. Pride had then steadfastly denied her a prodigal's return. They needed each other then and had been good for each other ever since.

'I'm terribly sorry Madam but I can't let you have this'.

Marie looked up from her reverie, slightly startled to see the postal clerk holding a large envelope in one hand and her postal notification in the other.

'Sorry, I don't understand' she blurted.

'This is registered mail Madam – it needs the addressee's signature and that's a Commander Peter Martyn. You need to get him to collect it or have him sign the authority for you to act as his agent'.

'But he's at sea' she protested.

'Sorry Madam, but we have to abide by the rules: we will keep it here for ten days so you have plenty of time'.

'Oh, I suppose so' Marie shrugged, 'thanks anyway'".

By now the twins were becoming positively fractious and so Marie wasted no time in collecting the shopping trolley and racing along to the greengrocers for the requisite 'Fred food' of lettuce, cabbage and carrot seconds. With that carton precariously balanced on top of the grocery trolley and the girls in tow she made a relieved exit for the car. Loading the car was simple, determining who should keep the dollar coin retrieved from the returned trolley was going to be less so.

'I will decide who gets the dollar depending on who is better behaved on the way home' was all that a stressed Marie could conjure up by way of Solomon's wisdom. 'Don't forget Daddy will be home tomorrow so you both have some tidying up to do'.

The ten-minute drive home from the shopping centre went peacefully enough, although Marie detected definite signs of elbowing in the rear seat as each dollar-contestant sought to have the other openly break the competitive truce. There was an overt and mutual breach, though, as soon as the boot was opened and each girl claimed carriage of the 'Fred food'. Unsure whether she would be seen as impartial umpire or as simply giving in, Marie adopted her benevolent motherly tone.

'If you two ladies will work together and both carry the carton through the side gate then I'm sure Fred would be very grateful and you could share the dollar.' That worked beautifully. Each girl attached herself to one end of the carton and happily skipped off to feed the rabbit at the end of the garden whilst Marie set about unloading groceries.

Deadlocked front doors were never designed to be opened easily by mothers carrying a miscellany of bags and packages. Juggling bags in one hand and the key in the other, Marie carefully tripped the lock and turned the door handle. She detected what seemed oddly like the odour of spilled fuel or gas. These were the last sensations Marie Martyn would ever experience on this earth. First the doorway was transformed into a destructive blast of overpressure, then the whole house exploded in a fiery detonation that shattered the structure and everything in it completely and irrevocably.

# CHAPTER 4

The duty Fleet Staff Officer received a telephone call from a Detective-Inspector of the Serious Crimes Squad at 7.15pm, just as the Sydney media was wrapping up the local evening news. Midway through most bulletins had been the story of some mysterious gas explosion destroying a house in suburban Little Bay. The story was complete with video of myriads of flashing lights from emergency vehicles but was light on detail and did little to excite much public interest. The Admiral was reached by telephone at home a few minutes later. At 7.40pm Petty Officer Daniel Charles, the signals yeoman aboard 'Succeed' knocked discreetly on his captain's cabin door and stepped inside.

'Immediate signal from Fleet, Sir' reported PO Charles, stepping forward towards the two officers seated at the tiny dinner table and passing across the clipboard with its attached teletype.

Pete Martyn scanned the sheet, looked up thoughtfully for a brief moment and passed it silently across to his deputy. Reaching backwards he pressed the Bridge intercom and told the Watch Officer to increase speed to 26 knots 'and get the navigator and engineer to come to my cabin also please'.

'Thanks PO' he continued to the yeoman. 'The navigator will give you an ETA as soon as he can. Reply as soon as you have it'.

'Odd, to say the least' observed Dave, and continued reading aloud 'ceremonial entry and all other scheduled activities tomorrow cancelled. Make best speed for Sydney and report ETA'.

'Oh shit!' exclaimed Pete. 'Sorry' he apologized to his startled deputy 'I've just realized that at this speed we are likely to reach the Heads in about five hours so that means berthing around

1AM. The troops will love that! Anyway, we had best put what's left of dinner in the warmer so we can get organized. Please let the troops know as soon as possible'

The navigator's ETA had rather more precision: 0125. As the berthing lines went across to Fleet Base at exactly that time, he pointedly looked at his watch with self-satisfaction. 'The Admiral is on the wharf Sir, should be impressed: perfect ETA, perfect alongside'.

'Thanks Pilot.' Pete gave a weak smile and continued quietly 'I'm a little more concerned, though, about that bevy of police and welfare types he's got with him. I'm going down to the quarterdeck to meet the Admiral. Ring off main engines but tell the engineer to stay at immediate notice for sea until I find out what's going on'.

Pete's uncle, Rear Admiral Usher, got straight to the point as the small group crowded into the captain's cabin. 'Peter, this is Federal Agent Garry Walsh from the AFP, Sergeant Johansson of NSW Police and you know Chaplain Jones and Mrs Palmer'. Nods were exchanged and the Admiral continued 'best sit down Peter, I'm afraid it's rather bad news'.

The next ten minutes passed in what Pete would only later recall as a blur. The news of his wife's death hit like a hammer blow and he couldn't help thinking that this was some sort of bad dream that would soon go away. His beloved twins were apparently not badly hurt but had been taken to hospital with shock, minor lacerations from flying debris and some hearing loss. Mrs Palmer, the Fleet Welfare Coordinator, would be looking after them temporarily the Admiral said, and he would be getting to see them himself 'shortly'.

'The entire Fleet staff resource is available for anything you might need Peter, and of course you have all our sincere condolences' the Admiral said uncomfortably. 'You have my mobile number for anything at any time, and these are the other numbers you might need' he added as he pressed a hand-written note into Pete's hands. 'Agent Walsh has a car waiting now to take you to see the children and he's going to stick with you for a while. I have arranged for the Chief-of-Staff to brief your XO on matters.

Pete would later remember being both shocked and confused. 'I don't quite see the AFP's involvement with a gas explosion' he had queried.

'Just a routine precaution Sir', Agent Walsh proffered, 'there are some unusual circumstances, but nothing to concern yourself with right now. We won't be taking any unnecessary chances with anything until we get a clearer picture of what has happened.'

The word 'terrorism' had sprung uninvited into Pete's head just then but he let it go and stood, looking pointedly at the federal agent with a 'shall we go?' look on his face.

'We will probably have a few questions for you later Commander' – this from the NSW Police sergeant – 'but for now please take my card and give me a call if you need any assistance. I will be keeping in touch with Agent Walsh and we'll organize something in the next day or so'.

Agent Walsh took his cue from that and they all filed slowly out of the cabin and off the ship.

........................................................

The hospital had been bad enough. This chapel situation looked like being something much worse. Pete had arrived early for the funeral together with his recently acquired shadow Garry. He had been somewhat surprised to be confronted by an armed AFP officer in what looked like full combat gear. Others, similarly dressed, were visible in the chapel grounds.

'Don't worry about it – just being careful' said Garry as he flashed his identification at the other officer.

They had become almost friends now, Garry and himself. A few home truths expressed on the way to the hospital nearly a week previously had cleared the air and set a basis for honesty between them.

'You need to know straight up Commander', Garry had said, 'initial indications from the Fire Brigade are that this was no accident. The house was full of accelerant residue with some sort of triggering device near the front doorway. We won't know the full picture until the forensic people do their stuff, but there are two glaring possibilities. Either we have a terrorism-related activity aimed at you and/or your family or someone was specifically targeting your wife. There are big differences as far as you are concerned: if terrorism then you are a victim; if the other then I'm afraid you are a suspect.

'Me?' Pete had protested, too tired to be truly angry.

'Why not?' was the response. 'You wouldn't be the first person to hire someone to dispose of his wife while establishing a clear alibi.'

There were more hard truths later and over ensuing days. His request to see his late wife had generated only awkwardness. There simply wasn't a body left to see. The girls themselves had been, and remained, badly scared but were physically sound and even their eardrums had remained intact. The flexibility of youth as the ER doctor had put it. A key issue was that he had nowhere to house them on discharge. He had almost said 'let's go home' to the twins before the realization hit that he had no home to go to. Equally, he had no car to take them anywhere – the police had impounded that. Doreen Palmer turned out to be a ministering angel, coolly advising that she had fixed up short-term accommodation for the girls with another Navy family and a suburban motel nearby for himself. That had triggered a further realization – he had virtually no money, few civilian clothes and no records, financial or otherwise. Apart from his fortnightly salary, most of which went straight into his wife's account, he was broke!

A light at the end of the tunnel appeared some days later in the form of a call from an insurance assessor. He had known he had household insurance but no evidence, so full marks to the insurance company for coming forward, he thought. Short-lived hope that was though! As the assessor politely explained, the police were treating the whole incident as a possible act of terrorism.

'As I'm sure you will be aware Mr Martyn, all our policies,

indeed those of all reputable insurance companies, carry an exclusion clause for acts of war or terrorism. We will remain', he added with only the slightest hint of embarrassment, 'unable to finalize any settlement until that aspect is resolved.'

So, broke and feeling very alone! Pete had always considered, when he had ever bothered to take time to think about it, that he was a fairly self-sufficient human being. That had been more so since the betrayal by his brother. Even in marriage, Marie and he had shared many things, including love, but without seeming to detract from his own sense of psychological independence. But Oh, how the mighty had fallen! From master of all he surveyed onboard ship to now feeling as alone and powerless as never before. Even Garry was apparently abandoning him for other duties on the morrow.

Loneliness is about to be even more emphasized here, Pete thought as he surveyed the scene in the chapel. Doreen had kindly brought the twins and they sat silently with him in an otherwise empty pew. He felt enormous gratitude to the Admiral who, in a dark suit for the occasion, sat behind with his graceful and well-dressed wife. The rest of the right-hand side of the church was almost entirely empty excepting for an expensively dressed older man who now made his way to the front and leaned over.

'Please accept my condolences Sir, here is my card' he murmured quietly, 'I wish to acknowledge your kindness to my son. If there is anything you ever need, anything at all, simply call'.

Pete smiled his thanks, though somewhat perplexed, and glanced at the card – 'Samuel Goldman, Financier'. He slipped the card into his pocket and thought no more about it.

Marie's parents and the extended Melbourne tribe as he had come to think of them, were of traditional Catholic stock. They had filled the left-hand side of the chapel and studiously ignored him as they had done since arriving in Sydney. He was not only the initial cause of Marie's exile from her 'proper' home but probably the cause of her death.

Pete's sense of isolation was oddly enhanced by the full-size coffin placed conspicuously in front of the altar. He knew it was virtually empty – which was pretty much the way he felt himself. Then something extraordinary happened. As the priest looked up to open proceedings there was noise and bustle at the chapel doors. A whole mass of smartly dressed men and women began to make their way up the aisle and fill the pews behind him. At first he thought there must have been a mix-up in bookings for the chapel, but as he turned to watch he started to recognize faces. Almost the entire ship's company had turned up to pay their respects – 120 quiet moral supporters of whom he was suddenly enormously proud. Maybe he wasn't alone!

Commander Peter Martyn hugged his daughters close and began silently weeping.

# CHAPTER 5

In a room not far away was another person weeping quietly. A young Filipino girl was checking her bruised face in the mirror after having had a very hard night. She knew her escort business had associated risks but the burly guy from the previous night had terrified her. He had only left after another violent bout of sex and his insisting on her cooking him breakfast. It had all started simply enough when she had tried to insist on him using a condom.

'No, no, I don't do natural – not allowed: I take care of health' she had pleaded.

Two ferocious back-handers across the face made the guy's intentions clear.

'You'll do what I want you to girlie, so let's get on with it eh?'

She knew she should have called the Police, he was rough and violent, but she was simply too scared. Even when he had fallen into a seemingly deep sleep, snoring loudly, she had remained almost frozen. He had left after throwing $1,000 cash on the breakfast table and then she thought once more about reporting him. No-one should have to put up with that stuff, she thought angrily, but really what was the point. She applied more make-up and checked her voice-mail.

......................................................

Ivor Slavinski was also checking his phone just then.

'Wharf Inn. Can U make 2pm?' read the incoming text.

A quick glance at his Rolex and a call to FlightLink reservations for a 10am flight would get him into Coffs Harbour before 11.30 and that would be plenty of time to assess the vessel and have a good lunch.

'OK' was his simple text response as, dressed in his newly acquired jeans, 'flannie' and sneakers, he hailed a taxi for the airport. A straightforward flight had him in Coffs on time and he alighted from another short taxi ride at the harbour. Coffs Harbour International Port read the large sign above the port building, although to look at the dilapidated state of the place one would imagine it a rustic backwater. Just as tired-looking was the object of his visit: a 48-foot timber offshore fishing trawler with 'Sea Urchin' barely legible on the bow. 'Jeez, I could buy this crap-heap with the loose change in my pocket' he mused. 'Still', his thoughts progressed, 'she's not the sort to attract too much unwanted attention'. With that he headed off for a short stroll up the hill to the Wharf Inn.

There is a wide perception that seamen the world over are a fairly rough and ready lot. That perception would have been strongly reinforced with one look at the seedy crowd littered around the bar of the Wharf Inn that day. An example was the gangly 'salt' sitting alone in a corner table nursing a schooner of beer. This was Greg, cook and rouseabout on the 'Sea Urchin'. Seeing Ivor heading towards him he almost cowered into his seat and avoided eye contact.

'Go get me a beer' ordered Ivor.

With a hurt look, but without a murmur of dissent, Greg did just that.

'So, what's up? Why the fall-off in orders?' questioned Ivor eyeing both Greg and his beer with equal distaste.

'Looks like they've starting making their own' responded Greg. 'Not sure exactly where, but see that guy in the blue jumper leaning against the end of the bar?' Without looking up or awaiting any response he continued 'that's Bluey. He's the fixer and he will head off to the lab to check on progress as soon as he's had his fill here'.

'Good: leave this to me', muttered Ivor as he slid a bulging envelope across the table. An envelope that disappeared into Greg's pocket in a flash.

The ensuing stony silence at their table stretched into a good fifteen minutes before 'blue jumper' eventually slapped the bartop and departed. Ivor casually rose and left through a second door. Ivor followed cautiously but 'blue jumper' evidently had no notion of being watched and walked for barely five minutes before entering a very ordinary suburban house. Ordinary that is until Ivor noted the heavily curtained windows and mounted security cameras at each corner. He continued past without obviously looking other than as a guy out on an afternoon stroll. Rounding the corner of the street he headed downhill again to the local service station.

'I need some four-stroke for the mower, you got any cans' queried Ivor.

The attendant simply nodded toward one corner, said 'pay when you've filled up' and went back to whatever occupied him on his phone.

Ivor filled-up, paid the bill and grabbed a cleaning rag from the driveway on his way out. This was no time for pussy-footing around he thought as he stretched his legs on the upward climb to his target. These guys were amateurs and on a sunny day like today would be quite relaxed. They thought they had good reason to be confident. He was right. It was a matter of seconds to knock two panels out of the paling back fence; another 10 seconds to make the few metres to the heavily curtained back window. A handy rock sorted the glass and the fuel was into the curtains and inner house in a simple pour. Kneeling to touch a light to his petrol-soaked rag he balled that up and pushed it through the broken window. Back to the fence and he had vanished into the back streets before the lab people could do anything about it.

Having listened with satisfaction to the sound of multiple sirens, he checked into a local motel. He paid upfront to ease the evident concern of the receptionist's suspicion of this newcomer with no car or baggage. A shower, something to eat and a dreamless night's sleep, thought Ivor.

...................................................

Ivor's dreams may have been somewhat disturbed had he been

aware of Magda. Magda was a Sydney social worker who often called in on her previous client, now friend, the young Filipino hooker. Magda was the sort of woman that took no prisoners. One look at the distressed, now very deep blue-black, face of her friend and she swore a series of expletives against men in general and the cause of her friend's pain in particular. 'You're coming with me', she asserted 'we are off to see my friends at the local station. By station she meant the police station, which is where they arrived after a short walk.

The Duty Sergeant was all process and little outward empathy. 'Take a seat over there' he said without preliminaries. They could then hear him speaking into an intercom.

'Karen, could you come out front please, looks like you have a DV'.

'DV means domestic violence' Magda explained to her charge, but before she could clarify anything with the Sergeant a smartly dressed woman arrived and invited them to follow her to a small interview room. Once they were all seated, she explained 'I am Detective Constable Karen Williams, please relax and tell me what's been going on'. Magda did most of the explaining before the young Filipino took up the story and Karen listened politely. Mentally she was counting the wasted minutes: sexual assault on a paid hooker was not going to attract too many investigative resources and common assault with no obvious suspect was similarly headed for the back shelf. She tried, though!

'Please describe the man in as much detail as you can', she requested.

Tall – 2 metres – heavily built, dark brown eyes, cropped hair, the tattoo of a knife of some sort on his left arm, flashy watch, spoke with European accent. All this went on her record as the interview continued.

'How was he dressed?'

'Smart, slightly rumpled grey suit – at least when he arrived.'

'Could you explain that for me please', Karen asked.

'He arrived in a suit but before leaving he took some clothes out of a shopping bag and dressed in those. There were blue jeans, a red shirt and sneakers'

'That's very good' noted Karen. 'Anything else you can think of: anything at all?'

'Well, his shoes smelled funny, a sort of oily smell, I think it was petrol.'

Karen sat up so quickly she startled her two visitors. This girl may have smelled petrol, but Karen smelled promotion. Two minutes later she was on the phone to her boss and the oiled machinery of a professional force whirred into motion.

# CHAPTER 6

The most serious challenge that Peter Martyn faced was a composite of emotion and practicality – what to do with the twins and, indeed himself for that matter. Their Melbourne grandparents, both in their late seventies, were clearly unable to cope with twin four-year-olds. Marie's siblings had run for cover at the very notion of taking on an extra two mouths to feed. Rescue had come from an unexpected source. Audrey Fagin, well-off but bored Little Bay mother of a four-year-old herself and self-avowed soul-mate of Marie had made an unannounced visit to Doreen at Navy HQ. She promptly and gratuitously offered her services as temporary 'house-mother' for the girls and without any specific limits on duration. Pete wasn't in the habit of looking a gift-horse in the mouth but Doreen was. Thorough background checks, lots of meetings and a couple of house visits at which all seemed sweetness and light combined to prompt a quick agreement. That left his own intentions to be determined.

The Admiral had set aside their family relationship and had been quite blunt at his interview, despite the courtesies and coffee in his office.

'Peter, you have been relieved of your command. That is absolutely no reflection on yourself or your capabilities, but I simply can't risk a deployable asset being under the command of someone in such an uncertain domestic and emotional situation. I know it must be tempting for you to throw yourself into your work, but at what cost and for how long? You are due shore time anyway. We could conceivably find some ad hoc desk job for you to mark time for a while. Alternatively, you could get your teeth into something worthwhile, by which I mean that file sitting in your lap'

'The Glove' was revealing his iron fist, whether encased in velvet or otherwise. It was apparent what he wanted to happen and Pete was in no strong position to take an opposite view. By the same token, the 'Moresby File' had piqued his interest. Curiosity had combined with the absence of readily identifiable options and Pete had acceded to a short-term posting, ostensibly as Naval Adviser Papua-New Guinea.

'You will be locally responsive to the High Commissioner', but be under no illusions, your priority is to get to the bottom of your brother's disappearance. In that I expect you to be directly responsive to me but I will technically be out of the loop so you will need to be discreet. Now that's sorted I can happily inform you that your promotion to Acting Captain has been approved. You leave in ten days: good luck!'

On leaving the Admiral, Pete was surprised to get a phone call from Sergeant Johansson.

"Could you pop over to Central Police station Commander', the Sergeant queried 'we have some new information'.

'Certainly, I'm not far off now, assuming I can get a cab I could be there in about fifteen minutes'

'Good, see you soon, just ask for me at the front desk'.

As it transpired, the Sergeant was waiting for him in the station lobby and showed him into a nearby interview room. A surprise addition was Agent Walsh who greeted him cordially.

'I'll bring you up to date Commander', said Johansson, and without further ado listed the forensic evidence which included Semtex residue and which pointed to professional involvement. The interview then took an unexpected turn.

'You previously alluded to an estrangement between yourself and your brother', Johansson noted, 'I need you to be specific on the causes and depth of that situation'.

'I don't see that relationship having anything to do with this' protested Pete.

'That's for us to decide' said Johansson rather coldly, 'please remember that this is a murder investigation'.

'Ok, well it was a while ago and basically he stole my fiancée' summarized Pete, not happy at all about the way this discussion was proceeding.

'Was this antagonism mutual?' continued Johansson.

'I have no idea really; I haven't spoken to Andrew for years'

'Are you sure?' – this from Agent Walsh.

'Yes! What an odd question, of course I'm sure', Pete retorted rather crossly.

'Peter', Agent Walsh responded, 'we have information that leads us to believe that your brother might be in Sydney. This places a new complexion on matters.'

That Pete's surprise was patently genuine escaped neither police officer.

'You should perhaps be made aware that I have just accepted a posting to Port Moresby with the particular added task of shedding light on his disappearance. If he is actually here, that all seems rather pointless', mused Pete after a short pause.

'OK Commander, that's not a matter for us to determine. I would repeat though, that this is a murder investigation and that is police business, not Navy and not personal. You will tell us if you have any contact with or from your brother, won't you?' Sergeant Johansson queried as he stood without waiting for an answer. The interview was evidently concluded. Neither police officer mentioned the as-yet unidentified man in the grey suit sighted in a neighbour's security video and again in the record of an alleged assault that same day.

On leaving the station Pete made a quick phone call to the Admiral's mobile but was forced to leave a voice-mail.

'Sir, the police believe that Andrew could be in Sydney. That would rather make any investigations in Port Moresby rather futile. Could you let me know whether you still wish me to go ahead with the posting north please?'

It was half an hour before the Admiral returned his call.

'Peter, nothing in this world is impossible, but I would be seriously surprised if Andrew were here in Sydney. I have no doubt whatsoever that he would have called your aunt or myself if that were so and I've checked with Sandra and he hasn't. Stick to the plan, my boy, and we'll see where it takes us.'

..............................................

It was surprising how quickly things could happen once the wheels of bureaucracy were turning in unison to a common end. Within the week Pete had received full diplomatic credentials and passport, host country briefings and flight tickets, whilst also completing a command handover to newly promoted Acting Commander David Bell. He had managed a couple of visits to his daughters and now sat in quiet isolation once more in his hotel room. It was time to face his demons and he let his mind wander back as he sought to picture exactly what those were.

The feud and breaking of links with his brother were occasioned, as any male sceptic could have ventured, by a woman. But what a woman, Pete mused. Christine Connelly was the epitome of the classically desirable female: blonde, blue-eyed and slim with long toned legs and a smile to die for. Extrovert in public, she had been warm and considerate in their private moments and, to his genuine surprise, she seemed to want his company as much as he sought hers.

They had met at a party hosted by his more socially active younger brother and Pete had initially felt a little like an outsider. He had been taken in hand by Christine, clearly the life and soul of the party and who had promptly spilled a glass of red wine over him in a moment of particular exuberance. Apologies had progressed to real conversation and the discourse had revealed a serious side to her character that he would not have guessed at. She was a graphic designer and, at 27, with the professional world at her feet. Within a couple of weeks they had ended up in bed together. The outcome had been mutually very satisfactory. At the time Pete was spending more time at sea than ashore, running a patrol boat out of Sydney and had the use of only a tiny flat in the CBD. Still, it was convenient and he and Christine saw each other, albeit intermittently, for a couple of months until Pete asked her to marry him. She had agreed, although not quite as enthusiastically as he might have hoped. Their on-off relationship continued for a few more months until one evening he paid a visit on their uncle, only to find his brother there in his cups. The scene in the lounge-room was tense and Andrew close to tears.

'What's up?' Pete asked innocently.

'Christine lost the baby', responded their uncle quietly.

'What baby?' Pete exploded 'why wasn't I told – and where is Chris?'

'She's at my place, you idiot, and just so you know, the baby was mine' Andrew had shouted into what became a shocked silence. After a while he added by way of explanation 'She was with me way before she met you, and has happily been with me almost all the time you've been gallivanting off to sea like the fool you are!'

'You bastard!' That was all Pete could conjure up in response and had stormed out without another word. He had spoken to neither Andrew nor Christine since.

Apparently, the pair had married some months later but had since, as far as Pete was aware, remained childless. The years had dulled that pain, but not the sense of betrayal by his own brother.

# CHAPTER 7

Andrew Martyn was not having a good day – indeed he had not had one of those for a few days, probably three or four he thought. Time had blurred but had settled, although that was hardly the word, into a sort of routine. He was getting what seemed like twice daily visits from a burly and uncommunicative Islander-type. Each visit was short and simple: a bottle of water and more recently an almost indigestible nougat bar followed by a needle in the leg and back into the darkness. The noise of powerful diesels was incessant, as was the constant rolling and occasional pitching of the vessel he was clearly in. His mental state was also having a rollercoaster ride. Whatever was in that regular needle helped. It didn't ease his discomfort but at least for a while he felt more mentally alert.

During one of his periods of greater alertness he had tried to think back to how this saga had begun. He remembered a strange phone call from a sailor in Port Moresby.

'I'm ex-Leading Seaman: I know you from Manus', began his caller, apparently referring to Andrew's time some years previously at the PNGDF base on Manus Island.

'You need to see something on the boat I'm on', continued his caller, 'can you meet me at the harbour tonight?'

'I'm sorry, but I don't have the time tonight to drop everything simply to visit a boat, could you be more specific about what you want to meet about? Perhaps you could drop into the High Commission and see me here?' Andy had responded.

Agitation was immediately evident in the caller's voice.

'This very dangerous boss. They kill me if they find out I talk to you. You the only person who I trust to talk to on this' con-

FLAWED DIAMOND

tinued the caller. 'If you meet me Waterfront Place twenty hundred tonight, I show you. Aussie government need to know this.'

His unknown caller had captured Andy's interest.

'So, what is your name and, If I could make it, how would I recognize you?'

'No names boss, I'll recognize you. See you then: don't be late'. This followed by the click of the phone call ending.

Andy had been intrigued, but with violent 'Rascol' gangs taking advantage of any vulnerable looking people around darkened areas, Andy was not about to simply head to the waterfront at night on his own. He had called the staff assistant, an Army corporal, to see if he could drive him there that evening and wait while he investigated the scene. This occurred and Andy had met up with 'Nico', a Papuan chef from a sleek 72-foot motor cruiser moored nearby. She was a smart, though clearly well-worn, vessel named 'Blue Turtle'.

'Follow me', said Nico, 'but we need to be quick, I'm the boat guard tonight but the others may come back any time'. He had taken him below decks and shown him three timber cases which, when one had the lid lifted, revealed what looked like automatic rifles.

'These are going to Rabaul for transfer to a bunch of thugs in Bougainville' said Nico angrily, 'this not right'.

'You need to talk to the police' Andy had told him, whilst also getting out his phone and taking a series of hurried photographs.

Andy had left Nico on the yacht and gone back to the car without incident.

................................................

Andy's nostalgic reverie was disturbed by the hatch opening yet again and his surly Islander jailer, for that's how he thought of him, appeared silhouetted in the opening. Unusually, there was an additional face this time, that of an older man. It was the older man who spoke.

'We are about to go into port for fuel and supplies', he said. 'There is a chance that we will get boarded. If you behave and

45

stay completely silent for a few hours then I will arrange to make your life more comfortable. On the other hand, should you make any noise whatsoever whilst in port then Tomas here will happily cut your throat. Is that clear?'

There were not too many satisfactory responses available to that threat, so a mumbled 'OK' was all Andy could manage.

Other than being in no shape to argue, Andy was also in no condition to think up any sort of escape plan, let alone physically effect one. His hands were still tied but he could just reach the back of his head where a lump the size of a duck-egg was apparent. The inside of his head felt almost as foul as the inside of his mouth and he realized that his whole body stank. With no other obvious choice, he simply rolled on to his side and went to sleep.

He was woken by silence. Almost silence anyway! The noise of the engines had stopped but he could hear people walking around on the decks above and snippets of shouted conversations. He then picked up a single word, 'Bula', seemingly called from above to someone on shore. Good grief, he thought, recognizing the conventional Fijian greeting, I'm in Fiji! Bangs, taps and miscellaneous noises continued for about two hours as close as he could estimate. The engine noise then re-started and from the vessel's increased movement was evidently underway again. He resigned himself to more of his uncomfortable, smelly and noisy existence.

Light! Movement! The anticipated water and muesli bar didn't eventuate. Instead Andy was grabbed by the legs and hauled out of his confinement. Looking around groggily he realized that he was in what could only be the main cabin of the vessel and was facing the older man he had glimpsed earlier.

'You can call me Hemi', said the man. 'I don't know what you've done Mr Martyn, but you have certainly upset my Chief for some reason. My job is to get you to him, preferably in one piece. Now you can try and escape', he added waving his arm at the calm expanse of completely empty ocean. 'That way you can be useful fish food. Alternatively, you can give me your word not to try anything and we'll get you cleaned up. So, what's it to be?'

Andy was feeling nauseous and with a headache but the option of getting cleaned up was attractive. 'I give you my word not to try to escape', he muttered.

'Good! But make no mistake mister, if you interfere in any way with the operation of my boat, I'll shoot you in the blink of an eye. That's as well as cutting your balls off and stuffing them down your throat.'

Hemi nodded to the larger guy, apparently named Tomas, who walked him out onto the after deck and ordered 'strip'. Having done so, he was shocked by a hosed stream of sea water and almost fell over. He guessed that constituted his 'clean-up' and was then thrown a pair of dark blue overalls.

'Get dressed and go see the skipper in the pilothouse', directed Tomas.

'You may as well make yourself useful while you're here', remarked Hemi turning away from the navigation screen in front of him. 'Can you cook?'

'Basics I suppose', responded Andy tentatively.

'Good, because our cook went AWOL so you can take over. But you look like shit so take one of these', he added, passing a small white pill. 'Don't worry, it won't kill you, but it should make you feel better. Now, go find the galley and I expect a meal for five by six-o-clock'.

Andy had obviously been dismissed so, barefoot and still damp from his hosing-down he went below and soon found what could only be the galley. The place was well-stocked and had excellent facilities so he set to work. Oddly enough, he felt much better after a few minutes, quite alert and with more energy. He gathered the makings for a simple steak and salad, found some plates and looked for some cutlery – which he found and eyed off the carving knife with a faint sense of hope. He parked that hope in the back of his mind and decided to toe the line for the time being and play chef.

......................................................

After a conventional breakfast on the fourth morning Andy's

duties looked like they were coming to an end. A low-lying island was visible on the horizon and they were clearly headed there. It was not long before they were pulling alongside a robust timber jetty marking what looked like the approaches to a luxury tropical resort minus the multi-storey buildings. Edged by white sands, crystal clear water and the occasional palm tree, the series of thatched bungalows and huts of a small village provided a vision of paradise.

'Where are we?' asked Andy politely of the boat skipper.

'Not something you need to know sunshine', was the surly response and Andy was bustled unceremoniously down the gangplank and up a well-worn pathway toward the village. Tomas had a firm hold on his collar and he was almost dragged to the front of a larger hut where he was forced to stop whilst Hemi went inside. He had little time to absorb his surroundings before he was thrust inside the hut and frog-marched to an upright cane chair.

'Sit' said a voice in the shadows to his front and an older man, looking to be in his early seventies, made his way into the open area of the hut and sat in a comfortable armchair. 'My name is Michael Sopolo. You can call me Chief', he added and, with a slightly deprecating wave of his arms, 'it is an honorary title. Now Commander, you have been meddling in affairs that don't concern you. I'm well aware of what you've been up to, there is just one little matter. What was in that registered letter you sent from Rabaul?"

'I have no idea what you are talking about', Andy started, and promptly received a solid whack across the back of the head from Tomas, who had evidently been standing just behind him.

'No protestations of innocence' spoke Sopolo, 'I mean that envelope for which you had a receipt in your jacket pocket. This one' he added, waving a small postal receipt slip in the air.

Andy had to think fast. 'Oh, that', he began 'that was just my expense sheets and receipts that I have to send in registered mail'. He had hardly finished when a second punch from Tomas almost knocked him off the chair. He decided to brazen it out and stared coldly at Sopolo.

'Mmmh, we will see', commented Sopolo almost to himself. 'Has he been taking his medicine?' He continued, looking past Andy to the back of the room.

Hemi answered simply, 'yes Chief'.

'When was the last one?'

'Before breakfast this morning' responded Hemi.

Sopolo looked pensive and gave Andy a smile that went nowhere near his eyes. 'Commander, you may conceivably be already aware that you are now almost certainly addicted to MDMA, which you might know better as Ecstasy. I have no doubt that you are feeling quite well and confident right now, but you won't by this evening. If you annoy me, I might just change the medicine to Ice, and that will certainly put you on a slippery slope you won't recover from. Take him away to reflect on his sins!'

Andy was pulled to his feet, marched off to a much smaller and empty hut at the edge of the village and dumped inside. He looked around but there was little to see until he saw what was obviously a guard of some sort silhouetted at the entrance. He had nothing to do except think and soon realized that there was little he could do about his situation. Escape might be feasible, but he had no idea where he was except that it was probably on an island somewhere in the Pacific. Equally, he had no money, no clothes and, he had to finally admit to himself, no plan. As the afternoon wore on, he also became increasingly anxious, confused and depressed. By the time he was collected at dusk, he was a bag of nerves and prepared to say whatever these people wanted to hear.

'Well Commander, have we thought some more about what was in that envelope?' Sopolo queried.

'It was a note to my brother in Sydney about what I was doing'.

'So why registered?'

Andy sighed deeply and unwittingly hung his head. 'I included a photograph of your crate of guns', was the reluctant response, 'and wanted to make sure he got it'.

'Now we are getting somewhere', said Sopolo happily and actually clapped. 'Honesty is always the best policy I find. I hesitate to disillusion you, though, but he will never be seeing that letter. That just leaves what is in your head and I will contemplate overnight about whether that stays on your shoulders. Meanwhile, Tamika will look after you. Until tomorrow!'

Andy looked up to see an attractive young island girl beckoning and, as he lurched from of his seat, she took his hand and led him outside. She kept hold of his hand whilst heading for another small hut, though this time furnished, albeit sparingly. There was a futon-style bed and side table with a simple screen across the doorway.

'Tamika?' he asked, looking up from the bed.

'Yes, I'm Tamika and I will be looking after you tonight' she responded smiling brightly. 'You lie there while I get some food.'

Tamika left and returned shortly afterward with a bowl of what looked and smelled like chicken and rice. She also had a glass of water and a pill which she insisted that he swallow first. That all done, he lay down and drifted off to sleep.

# CHAPTER 8

Acting-Captain Peter Martyn rather tentatively took his seat on QANTAS Flight 444 to Port Moresby without being entirely sure how, in a metaphorical sense, he had got here. The past three weeks had vanished in a blur of administrative arrangements and an emotional roller-coaster he would be happy never to repeat. The AFP had decided that there was no perceived need for ongoing personal protection. The forensics experts had identified Semtex residue in the rubble of his house and determined that, despite a moderate degree of technical sophistication being involved, it was probably not terrorism related. The ultimate purpose and origin remained a mystery. Sergeant Johansson of the local police had quizzed him for hours about possible family enemies and had kept him on the suspect list, which now included only he and his brother.

'Have you selected a main course, Sir', the voice of middle-aged male steward returned him to the present. Pete reached for the menu, fired off his choices and shortly afterward sat forward to engage with a meal he was sure could have been manufactured from extruded plastic. The wine, though, he both enjoyed and drank with determination so as to ease the prospective burden of going through the Admiral's 'Moresby File' for the umpteenth time.

There were really only a few sheets of relevance in the slim folder he had come to regard as his personal enigma. The first of these was a copy of Andrew's annual personnel evaluation from just four months previously. Signed by his Head of Defence Staff and countersigned by the High Commissioner, it was a glowing endorsement. He had achieved outstanding results in establishing a collaborative liaison with PNG Defence officials: his reports were precise, factual and well-constructed; and he had generally conducted himself in exemplary fashion. The rot seemed to have set in shortly thereafter and it was apparently a fairly rapid fall from grace.

Internal High Commission file notes recorded a series of complaints about missed appointments; a censure from the Deputy Commissioner for slovenly dress and behaviour; a second-hand report of domestic abuse verging on violence; and an incident of 'gross intoxication' after a local embassy reception. The *'piece de resistance',* though, was a police report of a foreign sailor's knifed body being recovered from Port Moresby's outer harbour. Andrew's business card had been found in the deceased's trouser pocket, together with a small packet of cocaine. Particularly damning was a witness report of the sailor arguing with a person matching Andrew's description earlier that evening. On the day after the body had been found Andrew had apparently boarded a civil flight to Rabaul on the eastern side of the country for an 'unauthorized facilities inspection'. He had not been heard from since. Whilst no arrest warrant had yet been issued, the PNG constabulary was particularly keen to interview him.

These reports, Pete couldn't help thinking, were about as indigestible as airline food. A wave of the hand, a bright smile and another glass of robust red eased the problem though, and Pete drifted off into an uneasy sleep until required to change planes at Cairns. Another dull flight of an hour and a half saw them landing safely in Port Moresby. Leaving the plane Pete was hit by a wall of heat and humidity and he idly wondered why the tarmac wasn't melting as he walked slowly to the terminal. 'This is worse than the Middle East', he thought, 'at least we had the ocean breeze there most of the time'. His diplomatic passport was fairly casually stamped until the immigration officer took a double check at the name and face. A button of some sort was obviously pressed because two badge-wielding plain clothes officers arrived within moments and asked him to accompany them to an office.

'Mr Martyn', one officer began, 'are you by any chance related to an Andrew Martyn?'

'I'm his brother', was the simple response, whilst wondering where this might be leading.

'Mr Martyn, the authorities here are very anxious to speak with your brother. Please tell us what you know of his whereabouts'.

Pete put on his innocent but worried face and responded honestly 'I have no idea. I have heard that he has gone missing but I have no further information about him, nor received any advice as to where he might have gone. I am hoping to discover what has happened myself. Is there anything you can tell me that might help?'

The officers glanced at each other and perceptibly shrugged. 'We can't divulge any such information at this stage, Mr Martyn', the lead officer said - rather pompously – 'but if you do hear from him or of information about where he might be, it is important that you let him know that it is in his best interests, and yours, to contact us.'

Pete gave a tired smile. He was getting rather used to police interviews lately and realized that being cooperative but largely silent tended to smooth their progress. He was evidently free to go and one of the officers escorted him to the arrivals hall where he collected his limited baggage. A uniformed Army corporal holding a name placard solved the problem of where to go next and he was collected with a welcoming smile. A slim, dark-skinned and simply dressed brunette, probably mid-thirties he thought, was with the corporal and introduced herself.

'I'm Angela, your PA' she said 'welcome to Port Moresby. Is that all your baggage?' she added with a surprised look at his fairly small and only suitcase. Pete nodded as she continued, 'accommodation or office?'

'Oh, I think accommodation please, I need to get cleaned up and a bit organized. I also need to go clothes shopping fairly soon', he added.

He was led to a car where Angela proceeded to issue a string of pieces of information and advice. 'You have been put into the Stanley Hotel to start with, duration depending upon whether you end up moving into the single-mans' quarters or your brother's accommodation. The Stanley is not bad and it's only a short walk from the High Commission. Not at night though! If you need to move around at night please get one of us to drive you – Corporal Ben, here, loves squiring us Defence types around in the middle of the night, don't you Ben?' This unsurprisingly met with a rolling of the eyes from Ben.

After a quick shower in his 'executive' room and wearing his uniform bush jacket with its shiny new Captain's epaulettes, Pete headed down to the equally shiny reception area and met up with Ben who whisked him off to the High Commission.

'Don't look around, but you're being followed', said Ben as he parked the car. 'Nothing much I can do about that', responded Pete, 'thanks for the lift.' Putting on a confident air, largely to mask his feeling of nervous anticipation he headed up to his assigned office to be met by a smiling Angela.

'First stop the Colonel, Sir', said Angela brightly. 'His office is next but one along the corridor'.

'Hey, welcome', breezed Colonel Duncan the Defence Adviser, 'terribly sorry about your loss Peter, you've been having a tough time of it with that and your brother's disappearance. I hope you can settle in for a bit, but I had an interesting phone call from the Maritime Commander the other day, who I gather is your uncle. Anyway, as I said, I hope you can settle in for a bit: we are the same rank so just let me know of anything substantial and I'll mainly leave you alone to get on with whatever. By the way, we rarely wear uniform around here except for formal occasions so you will find us all pretty relaxed. Well, there are some exceptions to that', he added raising his eyes to the upper storey.

'Actually, I don't have too many options right now', Pete responded, 'most of my clothing went up with our house, so I just have what came off the ship. But thank you for your thoughts. I was hoping to head into town and scare up some new gear.'

'You do whatever you need to old son' the Colonel replied affably, 'take whatever time you need'.

Pete returned to his office reassured and explained his clothing needs to Angela.

'Leave it with me for a while', she said, 'but first the Deputy High Commissioner wants to see you. Upstairs, end of the corridor', she added.

Pete found the required office and was met by a young receptionist.

'I'll let him know you're here', she offered, 'please a take a seat Captain.'

Pete sat and waited: and waited. After nearly fifteen minutes waiting, Pete decided that there was some sort of power play going on and simply left. He had been back in his office no more than a minute when the Deputy's receptionist burst in looking decidedly flustered. She managed a wan smile before 'He wants to see you now', she said breathlessly, 'and he's ropable'.

This time there was no delay. Pete went into the office and was confronted by what he later thought was a caricature of a 1960's office clerk. Pink shirt with an unmatched red bow-tie, narrow neck, goatee beard and hair parted in the middle.

The Deputy launched straight into a tirade. 'I see you have no diplomatic experience, so I'll explain. The High Commissioner is a political appointment, so I run this post. I'm your boss: if I summon you then you come and if you have to wait then you wait. We've had quite enough with that disgraceful brother of yours embarrassing himself and the High Commission with his antics, and we'll have no more of it. You defence types think you're a law unto yourselves: and you're not. Consider yourself on probation – and you haven't got off to a very good start', he ended in almost apoplectic fashion.

Pete hadn't been spoken to like that for over twenty years and found himself gritting his teeth. Rather than say anything at all, he simply left.

'Come with me, Sir', greeted the unflappable Angela sympathetically, 'we're going shopping'.

Sure enough, that's what they did. Into the main shopping mall escorted by the watchful corporal Ben, they bounced between menswear shops until he had quite a collection of bags. Dropping him off at the hotel, Ben whispered 'you're still being followed Sir, but its ok, I think it's the police just keeping an eye on you.'

'Thanks Corporal, I think I'll just grab myself a beer, don't suppose you would like to join me?'

'Love to Sir, but another time. Can't drink and drive as they say', and Ben departed with a cheery smile.

Pete was spoiled for choice in terms of bars and restaurants, but had been given access to the Executive Lounge, so headed up to the fifth floor and was greeted by a plush bar and casual eatery. He glanced around at the few business types sipping away and wandered toward a quiet corner. He stopped midstride. There, sitting alone at a table was an old NATO colleague Arno Vineberg.

'Arno', he called heading towards his old friend, 'fancy meeting you here'.

Arno looked startled, but recognition lit his face and he rather awkwardly got to his feet and they both smiled and shook hands.

'Greetings Pierre', exclaimed Arno, using his pet name for Pete from his days on secondment to the Dutch Navy whilst on NATO duties. 'What brings you to this part of the world?'

'I've just arrived as the new Navy man here', explained Pete, 'but I need a drink first, what's yours?'

'Off the booze at the moment Pierre', he responded sadly whilst pointing to the briefcase discreetly handcuffed to his left wrist, 'but this deserves a toast, so I'll join you with an OJ'.

Settled over drinks, the pair reminisced about miserable times in the North Sea and chatted amiably for a while. In a brief lull in the conversation, Pete waved at the briefcase: 'so what's this all about?' he asked politely.

'Oh, I work for a small Dutch company that provides envoys to some of the Belgian bourses, Arno explained, 'I'm really just a glorified courier but the company seems to like retired officers and I get to travel the world delivering the stuff'.

'Stuff?', Pete queried with raised eyebrows.

Arno looked around the room and lowered his voice. 'Diamonds', he advised cautiously. 'Sometimes the seriously high-value product but these are just loose industrial diamonds. Still, one has to be careful, even these would be worth a cool million. I do this run regularly after going through India'.

'I see the need for caution', Pete started, but was cut off as Arno waved to a smartly-dressed and attractive woman who had just entered the lounge.

'Sorry, here's my delivery contact now', Arno commented, standing up to greet his visitor.

Pete also stood and then froze in shock. Hair tied up in a bun, a slightly darker blonde these days, a few wrinkles around the face and a more relaxed stomach but still a very desirable woman. It was Christine! His sister-in-law stopped mid-stride and was clearly as disturbed by this unintended meeting as he was. She moved forward tentatively, shook hands with Arno and looked at them both.

'You two know each other?' she questioned as she sat, almost flopped, into the nearest spare armchair.

'From way back', Arno explained, 'we were in ships together as Lieutenants, drinking wine and saving the world. Still, let's do some business and I can relax then we can all share a toast', he added, passing a docket to Christine. She signed his docket and took the briefcase as Arno undid the handcuffs and passed both cuffs and keys across the table.

'All good', Christine observed, 'but I can't stay. It is good to see you again Arno, she smiled, then looked sadly at Pete. 'I'm so sorry to hear about your wife, Peter, I suppose we will need to get together to sort a few things out between us. Why don't you call around to our quarters when you're settled?'

'I would like that', Pete responded and stood as they shook

hands politely. He felt the warmth in her hand, but less so in her voice. He was shaken by this encounter and trying not to show it. That woman would always give his emotions a work-out, he thought.

'Small world', was Arno's only comment 'what was that about your wife?'

'She was killed in a house explosion a month ago' said Pete woodenly. 'Look, I'm bushed so I'm off for a bite to eat then to bed. Are you staying here?'

'Was, but I'm off on this evening's flight to Darwin then back home, old son; us worker-bees need to keep moving'.

'Pity, but great to see you Arno, it's been too long. How about handing over your business card and I'll try and stay in touch?'

'Good thinking, Pierre', replied Arno, 'sorry to hear about your wife', and the two parted ways.

# CHAPTER 9

Andrew woke to a bright, windless dawn and realized with some alarm that another body was in the bed with him. Tamika, completely naked, was sharing his futon and he sat up quickly trying to recall the events of the previous evening. That woke Tamika too, who stretched casually, pecked him on the cheek and got out of bed without the slightest hint of embarrassment.

'Time for some breakfast', Tamika noted looking outdoors 'please get dressed now and we go to food hall. Clothes on chair, shower at back of hut'. All this whilst clearly remaining very comfortable with her nudity.

'Did we? Er did I do anything last night.' Andy was mumbling, struggling to find the right words in his discomfort. He was met with a bright smile, a shrug and a slight shake of the head that spoke mainly of apparent disappointment.

By the time Andy had showered and dressed in the provided clothing: a simple t-shirt, shorts and sandals; Tamika was at the doorway dressed in a simple floral shift. She held out her hand for him to take and then follow. She led him to a large hut in the centre of the complex where he was astonished to find a very contemporary dining room, luxuriously fitted out and fairly crowded. His fellow diners were all relatively young, varying from early teenage to late-twenties and invariably relaxed and smiling. Apart from a few quick glances as he entered, he drew no particular attention, despite being the only European in the room. Meals were buffet style and he enjoyed a breakfast of eggs and toast as good as one would find in any high-end restaurant, although Tamika simply ate a small bowl of fruit. Then Tomas arrived.

Tomas was a large man with a no-nonsense attitude and if Andy's experiences on the boat were anything to go by, he had few social skills and absolutely no patience. Accordingly, when Tomas gestured for him to leave, he followed without demur. He was led back to the larger hut where he had first met Sopolo, the Chief. The latter was sitting as before in a large armchair, but this time there was a second chair nearby which he gestured to. With a nod from Sopolo, Tomas left. Andy took the proffered chair and looked more closely at his captor. Dark, almost glossy, black skin with a long greying beard and sharp half-closed black/brown eyes: clearly not a local Islander.

'Well, Commander', he began, 'let me explain a few things about your situation. You are on an island, which I control. It is an impossible swim to anywhere else. I can dispose of you or I can make use of you. So, which is it to be, I wonder?'

'I am obviously not in much of a position to debate the point', observed Andy drily, 'that's your call, but for equally obvious reasons I am not enthusiastic about being simply disposed of as you put it.'

'Ah, I see a glimmering of good sense', continued Sopolo. 'What do you know about global warming?'

Taken aback by this apparent change in direction, Andy had difficulty putting together a sensible response. 'I suppose it's happening' was all he could manage.

Sopolo became instantly agitated. 'But of course it's happening', he declared angrily, and that outburst seemed fueled by genuine feeling. 'Did you know that your industrial countries are pouring nearly a thousand tons of $CO_2$ into the air every second? Don't answer that, I'm being rhetorical. Global temperatures are rising alarmingly, glaciers are retreating, whole species are becoming extinct. Most significantly of all for us here, sea levels are steadily rising and typhoons becoming longer, more frequent and more ferocious. My people, by which I mean the Islanders, live on the coastal fringes of atolls which are sometimes only four metres above sea level at their highest point. If things keep going on as they are, and if your blind politicians continue their ignorant policies of denial then they certainly will, these islands will become progressively uninhabitable. So, what do you think we should be doing about that?' he finished, almost out of breath.

Andy realized that he was on thin ice and needed to tread carefully with what now seemed to him to be a fixated local tyrant. 'There doesn't seem much that you or I could do about it from an isolated island', he offered.

'That's where you're wrong, Commander, what I can and will do is save the Cook Islanders from extinction.' Sopolo paused, seemingly realizing that he had given more away than he intended.

'How?', Andy dared to challenge, wanting these revelations to continue.

'Education and land acquisition!' declared Sopolo. 'More of that later, he added, now tell me about yourself'.

Andy gave him a brief synopsis of his career, to which Sopolo listened intently.

'Maybe you can be of use' Sopolo said as he got up and started walking around the hut. 'Let me tell you about how this started and maybe you could come onboard for the ride. As you may have noticed, I am from Buka, born in a small town called Hahalis. My father was keen for local autonomy from a corrupt administration. He became involved with the Mataungan Movement based in Rabaul which was advocating independence. Your corrupt Colonial Administration declared them Communist agitators and then claimed people in Hahalis were running a Cargo Cult and 'Baby Farms'. All rubbish of course, but people died, including my father, and I vowed to continue that fight, starting in Bougainville. We succeeded there, at least partly, but I was forced to relocate and came here. You now know that we are in the Cook Islands, and I have come to love these people, who are the nicest anywhere on earth. I am determined to help and protect them.'

'How?' Again, Andy felt the need to challenge his captor.

'I told you, education and land acquisition', Sopolo said rather testily, 'every one of the young people you see here in this village has the opportunity for a fully paid education at an Australian university, followed by land ownership there, and their children will be Australian citizens'. Sopolo finished with a proud smile, although even then the smile did not reach his eyes.

'That sounds very ambitious, not to mention expensive', offered Andy.

'Yes, but I have an ace up my sleeve', Sopolo continued with evident pride. 'Diamonds!' He paused to watch Andy's reaction, which was patent surprise. 'There was no fresh water except rain water when I first came here', he explained, 'so I drilled for water along the East coast. We didn't find fresh water. What we did find was diamond-bearing volcanic rock, and after a couple of years of dedicated effort we can now recover and export modest quantities of industrial diamonds. But more of that later. I look forward to raising the level of intellectual conversation around here, so, to mark our new relationship, I will call you Andrew, and you can call me Chief.' He chuckled. 'For now, Andrew take a day or so to familiarize yourself with the village. I will then be inviting you to help with the education of our youngsters. Any questions?'

'What about those arms I saw?' Andy queried. 'I cannot be a party to arms smuggling.'

'Fear not, that was a one-off. I never forget my friends in Buka or the rest of Bougainville who simply wish to have the means to ensure their continued safety and autonomy. We are not arms traffickers!'

'Could you clarify the role of Tamika for me please?' Andy was uncertain how to phrase this potentially embarrassing question. 'I mean especially our sleeping arrangements.'

A loud guffaw followed from Sopolo, 'oh, you mean sex', he roared 'don't you worry about that. She will look after you in any way you want. If you get her pregnant, she will be even more delighted.'

With that, Tomas was summoned and a bemused Andy was

then immediately led back to his temporary (he hoped) abode. Tamika greeted him happily and declared that they would go on a tour of the village.

'So, what is this place called?' was Andy's first question.

Tamika replied with evident pride, 'this is Nivano', she informed him. 'The island is called Rakahanga, but my people call it Tapuahua. We are part of the islands named after your Captain Cook. I was born here and life is good, if sometimes a bit boring. You are the first excitement in my life for over a year.'

'Tamika', he ventured, 'why did the Chief think you would be happy to get pregnant?'

'Oh, then I get to go to Australia after all', she replied with another broad smile. 'I was hoping to go with my boyfriend many months ago but he died after a fishing accident when they couldn't get him to hospital in time.'

They continued to wander peacefully through the village together and Andy was mildly surprised that almost all the huts were of solid construction with steel roofing rather than the thatched grass huts he had come to expect of a Pacific island. In all other respects, though, it was typical tourist brochure stuff: coconut palms, breadfruit trees and intermingled pandanus edged by pure white sands and an ocean as blue as he had ever seen. That made him think of his predicament and he aimed toward the wharf where he had been offloaded. There was no vessel there and the wharf, such as it was, comprised only a few metres of mixed stone and concrete adjoining the more robust timber jetty that the cruiser Blue Turtle he had arrived on.

No harm in asking, he thought. 'Where is the boat I came on kept?'

'That only comes to deliver important goods for the mine', she said, 'other goods come by barge from the other islands.'

'So where is this mine you speak of', he risked asking.

'Other side of island', she replied innocently, 'but we are not allowed to go there for safety reasons. Anyway, now is time for meal' she added and headed off to the communal diner.

A filling meal of fish and Taro followed by a serve of Papaya rounded out their day and, as dusk began to descend, they made their way back to the hut. Tamika foraged around her goods and produced a tablet she insisted he take.

'I don't want to take this', Andy protested.

Tamika suddenly looked very concerned. 'You must', she declared, 'we get into big trouble if they find out you no take.'

Andy resigned himself to swallowing the pill and soon started to feel quite a bit less anxious and generally more alert. Meanwhile Tamika had slipped off her shift and stood before him naked once more and quite unashamed. He had to admire her body: long brown legs, smooth skin, pert breasts and a smile to die for. Maybe he would, he thought, die that is, but there was little doubt he was becoming strongly aroused and was feeling unusually uninhibited. He slipped off his clothing and Tamika was in his arms and kissing him before he could reach for her. They fell onto the futon together and began making love, gently but with increasing passion and energy. She demonstrated a remarkable skill in her love-making, so she was clearly no virgin, but Andy felt himself feeling something more than just sheer lust for this beautiful young girl. Those were his last thoughts before drifting into a tired and dreamless sleep.

# CHAPTER 10

Pete woke slowly in the unusual comfort of his hotel bed, sorted out some of his newly acquired clothing and, after a quick shower and breakfast, headed into the High Commission some five minutes away. His new office was clinical, with no outward sign of its previous occupant. He looked around for signs of his brother's existence and found none: no folders, pictures, notes or anything at all to suggest that he had once occupied this space. Oddly depressed, he sat and examined his in-tray that consisted of a small pile of news reports on PNGDF activities and not much else. He sat contemplating what to do next when Angela breezed in.

'You're early', Angela called cheerfully, 'we don't usually kick off until 0830. Is there anything special you would like seen to?'

'Angela, please come in and sit down.' Once she was settled, he continued cautiously, 'I need to find my brother. What can you tell me about him?'

'Well, he's missing to start with, and that's very unusual. He normally keeps me up to speed on all his movements and I keep his diary. There is nothing in that, I've looked over his planned schedule a million times and there is nothing unusual in it.'

'How about himself, how was he behaving? Anything unusual?'

'I don't like to gossip Captain, and that's certainly frowned on around here, but I can say he didn't seem himself after that meeting with the boat's chef that was drowned. I am pretty sure he was not having an easy time of it at home, but that had been the case for a while. The last day or two he was here was different: he seemed quite shaken up when he heard the news reports of the drowning.'

'So, what did he do? Did he say anything about it to you?'

'He had been listening to the local morning news and I heard him walking around the office saying "shit, shit, shit" to himself, then he asked me to nip out and get the morning paper. When he read that it sounded like he slammed the paper hard down on his desk, cursed a few more times and said he was off to see the Harbourmaster.'

'Thanks Angela, that's helpful. Anything else you can think of, please let me know. It looks like I need to meet the Harbourmaster myself, so could you see if a driver is available please?'

Fifteen minutes later Pete was seated in the Harbourmaster's office. The man looked like the old salt that he probably was and sucked on a long-stemmed pipe as he spoke.

'Sure, I remember the Commander', he affirmed, 'your brother you say. Don't suppose you could show me some sort of ID to prove that?' he asked.

That out of the way, Pete asked about the last time they had met.

'He wanted to know about that cruiser that was berthed at the main wharf. Blue something, I think. Yes, Blue Turtle' he read from a log he had on this desk, 'she had sailed for Rabaul the previous night, not sure what time exactly, the office wasn't manned.'

'Thanks. Anything unusual about that particular vessel?'

'Nothing that comes to mind really, she's a Cook Islander that doesn't come in often, maybe once a year. There is some speculation the guy they found floating the next day came from her but I wouldn't be too sure about that.'

Pete expressed his thanks and departed back to the office, not hopeful that anything he had discovered was useful. He looked up as he entered his office to find a tall, clean-cut stranger sitting on his desk.

'Ah the wanderer returns! Hi, I'm Phil Stroud your local friendly AFP man', he announced jumping down and offering his hand.

'Pleasure, I think' said Pete absently, 'I'm getting a bit edgy about police visits these days.'

'I suppose you have been going through the wars lately, and please accept my condolences on the loss of your wife. Garry Walsh in Sydney has put me in the picture about everything that happened down there and I have good news and not-so-good news' he said quite cheerfully. 'First, do you recognize this man?' He handed over two grainy photographs, one showing a man in a slightly crumpled grey suit walking down a footpath and the other of what seemed to be the same man but just head and shoulders.

Pete looked closely at the images then shook his head. 'I'm afraid I don't recognize him at all.'

The AFP officer was watching Pete's reaction very closely. 'OK, here's the thing. These shots are from a domestic security camera about five doors down and on the opposite side of the street to your old house. They were taken just before and others just after the explosion. We haven't yet identified the guy, but I expect we will in due course. Helping is an identikit from the NSW police that looks like the same guy who beat up a hooker the same evening and so they are after him too.'

'That's the good news, what's the not-so-good?' queried Pete after a short pause.

'Oh, well that still leaves you in the frame for possible payment of the killer', said Phil bluntly, 'how's your finances?'

'Not enough to finance a hit man even if I wanted to, that's for sure', responded Pete 'in fact I'm almost broke. I nearly maxed out my credit card getting new clothes yesterday.'

'Yep, we know: we checked', finished Phil as he looked almost sympathetically at Pete. He left with a friendly nod and a promise to keep in touch.

Pete was left feeling both frustrated and dejected after that conversation. His dark mood was interrupted by a cheery greeting from the door.

'Come on you poor soul, come and have a light lunch with your PA. I would expect you to shout but I heard part of that last conversation, so lunch is on me.'

With that, Angela took him along to the local eatery and they did indeed enjoy a light lunch together. Angela proved to be a personable lady and a good conversationalist who seemed to know everyone in and everything about the High Commission.

'I do seem to have got off on the wrong foot with the Deputy though', Pete remarked at one stage.

'Oh, don't worry about that oxygen thief', Angela had responded, 'your brother presented him with a tie once. It had an anchor with a big 'W' on top and he told him it was the world maritime tie. The Deputy wore it around for a couple of days until someone must have told him it stood for 'Wanker' and he never forgave the Commander'.

Back in the office Pete glumly sorted through some pieces of routine correspondence then thought he should face his demons and talk to his sister-in-law.

'Hi Chris, it's Peter' he began nervously when the phone answered. 'I thought we might meet up if you are comfortable with that.'

'Sure. Look, I won't eat you, why don't you come around for a spot of dinner? Say seven?'

Pete agreed and found himself surprisingly looking forward to the evening.

Nerves cut in again later as he knocked on her door. She seemed quite relaxed and welcoming though, and the first drink settled his butterflies. She was wearing a simple strapless black dress and low heels, looking, he thought, like the ravishing young woman he nearly married.

'So, what's the briefcase pick-up all about?' he asked toward the end of their meal, 'it was certainly a shock meeting you again like that.'

'What's a bored expat meant to do, Pete, I got a job. It's only picking up important documents and stuff for the mining companies, but at least it gives me something to do. It's all very well for Andy to be charging around the country doing whatever he does, but I'm stuck here in this place with no friends and nothing much else to do except the weekly shop. Andy's coldness didn't help and then he started drowning his sorrows in alcohol. I think he was having an affair with that secretary of his, Angela or whatever her name is.' She got up and reached into a drawer, pulling out a small bag of white powder. 'I also found this in his bedside cabinet. I think its cocaine.'

Pete felt both mildly astonished and quite sympathetic and proceeded to top up their glasses by way of distraction. He looked across the table at her as she resumed her place and probed cautiously, 'do you want to talk about what happened to us?'

She downed her wine and looked dismal 'Pete, I'm so sorry. That was the worst decision I have ever made, not marrying you. It was an awful time with you being away at sea so much and with Andy being so insistent. I was young: I kept going to his parties; he kept pushing and pushing and eventually I gave in and slept with him. Oh Pete, I'm so sorry. And then, of course I got pregnant. He insisted it must be his and I supposed he must be right. Oh God, I was such a mess', she finished, stood up and burst into tears. Pete leapt to his feet and went around to comfort her. He held her closely and smelled her, then brushed the tears away with his lips. Her lips came around to his and they were kissing, gently at first then more intently.

'Come', she said and led him around to the bedroom where they began frantically removing each other's clothes. 'God, I've missed you' were the only words spoken before they were making love. Pete thought little. He was in that rush of lust and excitement that comes from not having had a woman for a very long time. He sucked her breasts avidly whilst stroking her stomach and entered her quickly and forcefully. For her part she began moaning and raking her nails down his back with evident pleasure. They came together in a frantic burst of energy and then simply collapsed.

Both apparently replete, there were a few murmured sighs each and no conversation for quite a while.

'I had better get back to the hotel', Pete eventually muttered.

'You can't, it's dark and not safe. Stay!' was her sleepy response.

Pete was in no state or mood to argue and so stayed. They had pleasurable sex two or three times again until eventually stirred into more mundane action by the morning sun.

'I suppose you will want this house back', Chris commented during a toast and coffee breakfast. 'It's Andrew's entitlement for a Government quarter, not mine, so I guess I'll have to move.'

'No rush darling, we can sort that out in the fullness of time. But for now, I had better get back to the salt mines and put in a day's labour.'

He headed off to the office that morning feeling physically drained but mentally better than he had for a long time. His thoughts then turned with a stab of guilt to Marie and the twins. He would give Audrey Fagin a call as soon as he got into the office and maybe get to have a word with the girls. From nowhere obvious, the question then popped into his head as to how Chris knew that his wife had died. Parking that thought in the back of his mind he continued on to fulfil his day's duties.

# CHAPTER 11

Into a fairly nondescript office tower in Canberra an equally nondescript group of smartly dressed public servants entered, although separately. The lobby sign indicated that this was the location of the Attorney-General's Department. They each approached a second-floor 'secure' conference room, placing any computers on an adjacent table and mobile phones in a cabinet outside labelled for that purpose. Inside, they took their predetermined places and chatted amiably. Finally, an older, slightly corpulent, man entered and took his place at the head of the table. He was an Assistant Secretary of the Department of Prime Minister and Cabinet and, for this routine meeting at least, chaired the National Security and Intelligence Working Group.

There was not a lot on the agenda and no-one expected a long meeting. Events in the Middle-East were canvassed without argument or much discussion and the trade representative gave a summary of a number of contentious trade issues that were either potentially damaging or potentially beneficial to the national interest. Moving on to 'other business', the foreign affairs representative reported that his principal, that is the Minister for Foreign Affairs, had received a call from his New Zealand counterpart asking for diplomatic support. They were attempting to get the Cook Islands government to reconsider their suspension of NZDF surveillance flights over that country.

'Did they say what the suspension was all about?' queried the chairman.

'No, that what makes it more intriguing', responded the original speaker. 'As you know, the Cook Islands are self-governing but New Zealand has had an acknowledged responsibility for its defence and external security matters. They conduct routine fisheries surveillance flights over the area which are in the Cook Islanders' own interests and that has never previously been questioned'.

'Maybe I can add an element here', interjected the Defence representative. 'We have received formal advice that the Cook Islands have declared a twenty nautical mile 'no-fly' zone around one of their north-westerly islands. We have no official intelligence on why, but our NZ liaison officer believes it is something to do with a diamond mine they have established there.'

'Diamonds? Are you sure? That's all coral atoll country', added the trade representative.

The chairman looked bemused and questioned the group generally 'are we really sure that they could have established a diamond mine on one of their islands? Anyone?'

There followed blank looks and silence all around.

'Ok, let's set that aside for a closer look' decided the chairman, 'we need a gemologist or a geologist or someone like that who knows what they're taking about to give us an appraisal. Jonas', here he acknowledged the trade representative, 'and Defence, if you could add in anything you find to Jonas please. Meanwhile we will meet again the day after tomorrow to review what we have and see if we need to escalate this. Anything else gentlemen?'

Charles, the Federal Police representative added a small item. 'Our Chinese colleagues are cooperating again', he noted to the sound of a few chuckles, 'at least their Hong Kong element. We have been sent a preliminary alert note on a PRC vessel named the "Da Qing" which does a Shanghai, Hong Kong, Sydney run. Some suspicion of drugs involvement apparently but the significance is the Chinese cooperation.'

'That's good news, Charles', the chairman noted, 'while you're here, what's the latest on the possible terrorist threat associated with that Sydney explosion?'

'Downgraded to virtually nil', Charles responded. 'we are almost certain it was a single one-off and targeted attack.'

'Back on the Cook Islands for a second', the Immigration representative obviously wanted to add his pennies' worth, 'we've been getting a couple of queries about them buying up land in Queensland. Not enough for the foreign investments board to worry about, but the land is all going into the name of some Cook Islands charity supporting students. Intriguingly, all their female students are turning out to be pregnant. Nothing illegal about any of this, but just thought you should know as it's a bit unusual.'

'Thanks for all that, gentlemen, we'll reconvene day after tomorrow with whatever you can ascertain in the meantime.' The chairman closed the meeting and they all filed out.

................................................

48 hours later the Working Group reconvened. 'Jonas, you have the floor', declared the chairman.

Jonas got to his feet and pointed to a wall map of the South Pacific that had mysteriously appeared on the side wall. 'The Cook Islands', he started, 'often known as the diamond of the South Pacific, 5,000 kilometres east, comprising fifteen islands of which the capital is Avarua on Rarotonga in the south. We have a small but significant trade surplus, main imports here pearls and gems – not diamonds I might add. We have no strategic ties other than through New Zealand and the South Pacific Forum. New Zealand has the most influence and interest and China may have some interest as part of their 'belt and road' initiative. Our interest is simply because it lies within our acknowledged sphere of strategic interest. The place we are focused on is here', he pointed, 'the island of Rakahanga, relatively tiny and miles from anywhere. Supposedly discovered diamonds there some eighteen months ago and certainly advertising industrial diamonds and the occasional gemstone on the world market'.

'We have a geologist's report on the area, confirming a 100 percent coral atoll structure for the island concerned. Diamonds are almost entirely found in eroded volcanic pipes and igneous rock, by which I mean rock formed by liquified magma after it solidifies near the earth's surface. No-one will offer absolute certainty, but the scientific consensus is that the probability of finding diamonds in a coral atoll is less than 0.1 per cent.'

'So, if not discovered locally, where could these diamonds be coming from?' queried the chairman.

'There are over twenty countries mining diamonds, including our own Kimberly region', continued Jonas, 'but there are no reported sales to the Cook Islands. An alternative source is the 'conflict' or 'blood' diamond trade which involves unregulated smuggling of product, mainly out of Africa. Historical sources of those have been Angola, Sierra Leone or the Congo but that trade has been largely controlled over the past decade. There are also synthetic diamonds, mainly coming from China, but any gemologist worth their salt would be able to identify those.'

'So, where does that leave us?' The chairman's question hung in the air. He looked at Francis, acting for the Attorney-General's department which managed the secret intelligence services, 'Do we have any assets there?'

'You know I can't answer that', retorted Francis stonily.

'How about Defence?'

'We supplied a 40-metre Guardian Class patrol boat to the Cook Islands under our Pacific Patrol Boat Program, but they have their own people manning that now. So, I'm afraid the answer is no', responded the Defence representative.

The chairman looked thoughtful. 'So where does this leave us', he asked. 'Do we escalate?'

Francis looked around the table and spoke up somewhat reluctantly, 'I suggest we sit on this and monitor any developments', he said, 'we have no concrete evidence of any wrongdoing and if they don't want surveillance flights, that's really their business and New Zealand's.'

'Ok, that's what we will do', declared the chairman. 'We will keep the Cook Islands on the radar as an ongoing agenda item with no further action for the time being. Thank you, gentlemen, this meeting is closed.

# CHAPTER 12

Gazing from the Cooktown wharf at a sixteen metre fast Austal offshore fishing vessel, Ivor Slavinski felt a degree of pride in his fifty percent ownership of the vessel. He had bought out the previous part-owner when that man had foolishly declined his offer to pick up 'special' consignments from offshore. Not that he had paid any money, it was just that the person concerned had disappeared in mysterious circumstances after handing over an ownership receipt to Ivor. The other part-owner had seen the light and had been exceptionally cooperative for at least the past two years. He had also been well rewarded and lived in a degree of comfort he was loath to lose.

Ivor climbed on board whilst carefully avoiding the jumble of diving equipment and game fishing gear perpetually residing on the expansive aft deck. That display was deliberate: an attempt to allay any fears about the boat's proper role. Neither the skipper nor his casual offsider was evident, so Ivor checked out the boat thoroughly and satisfied himself all was in order. He then flicked the former a text message: 'in town, meet me at the boat one hour' and strolled off for a quick beer. Having come from down south he was feeling the heat. His thirst was quenched after a couple of schooners and he returned to the boat feeling somewhat cooler.

'Hey Anders, how's it going?' he shouted to the tall, rangy Swede who skippered the boat and had almost as few morals or scruples as he had himself. They shook hands like old colleagues and sat down in the cabin to discuss business.

'All good and smooth', said Anders, 'the pick-ups have been easy and we can get as far down the coast as we need, avoiding Cairns of course. There's too big a crowd of Customs people there. The market is as strong as ever, we could probably up the quantities on 'speed' if you want. 'Ecstasy' has been a bit patchy but we've got rid of all we've received. Money's in the bank.'

'I'm off north tomorrow to sort out the next sailing. Stay ready, stay focused, Anders and we'll keep doing well together. Just remember, loose lips sink ships!'

The pair parted company and Ivor jumped into his rental car and headed up through town to the North-West valley where the coastal scrub turned to lush green in a valley with a dusky mountain backdrop. He was getting tired and not really interested in the scenery, just getting the next visit over with. He was here to check on the progress of the Chief's new Aussie generation. He pulled into the entrance to a neat gated driveway, pressed the call-button and simply said 'Ivor'. The gate slid open and he drove toward a magnificent two-storey chalet in the Swiss style. He was met at the front door by a broad-shouldered and elderly Islander woman.

'I wasn't expecting you today', the lady almost spat. She clearly didn't like Ivor and, standing there with hands on hips, she was not about to make him feel too welcome.

'Thank you for your warm greetings Moana', he growled with deep sarcasm, 'don't forget who pays the bills around here. Let's see the books.'

'The Chief pays, not you', Moana retorted. 'This way.'

The pair made their way to a spacious office where Moana sat behind an oak desk and passed across a substantial ledger. 'There are twenty youngsters now, 11 girls and nine boys, plus the 3 staff here, she began. Most of the students are lodged in on-campus accommodation at the university in Cairns except for three girls who are too close to term. We have made arrangements with the local creche and kindergarten for next year, although they have upped their prices and that is stretching the budget. The bus has been a godsend for getting the kids down to Cairns and back each week so that was money well spent. First semester exams are due in a couple of weeks and the grades are all good so far; a couple getting 'distinctions', especially those doing environmental management. We have had no trouble except for two of the boys getting into fights with the locals but no damage was done and they have been put on stoppage of allowance for a while. I have bought six new urban houses, mostly in Cairns and one small piece of rural land. The houses are all rented out and the income paid into the Hahalis account, less the agent's costs of course. You'll see that all the accounts balance.'

That was a better summation of their situation than Ivor could have ever hoped to get from him reading the accounts, which was not his strong suit. He made a show of reading diligently but soon gave up and slid the ledger back to Moana.

'I want the Title Deeds' was his initial demand. He then attempted a pale imitation of a smile, 'I'll be staying the night. Are any of the girls here?'

'No, and don't you dare even think about it. You know very well that they are off-limits', Moana rebuked. 'Dinner will be in the dining room at six-thirty. There will just be the two of us. Janice will show you to your room', she finished as she rang a bell for the domestic assistant.

...................................................

Dinner had been almost as cold as the atmosphere in the room that evening, and Ivor had to console himself with a reasonable night's sleep in anticipation of an early start for Darwin then Hong Kong the following day. That day dawned almost as bright and balmy as his island home and Ivor mused on the ironic humour of the Chief in settling for Cooktown as their mainland base. He would probably like to see it renamed 'Cook Island Town' one day he thought cynically. He got back into his car pleased to be on his way with another box ticked. He had an hour's wait at the airport for his flight to Darwin and, when it finally boarded, he was none too happy about the tight seating in the relatively small aircraft.

After a continuous string of airline flights and a testy meeting with his Chinese contact in Hong Kong, his mood when he arrived back in Port Moresby was surly to say the least. He knocked firmly on the door of Christine Martyn, whom he knew as Chris Connelly. 'I need a drink first, then business' he said brusquely. That done, he spread himself into an armchair and passed across a folder. 'Put those away with the incoming shipment, they're Title Deeds', he demanded. 'Was the shipment correct? Have you weighed it yourself?' These and other practical business matters were addressed at almost machine-gun pace. He then waved his glass for another drink, but as she went to fetch it her mobile rang.

'Hi Chris, it's Pete. Would you like me to come over?'

'Oh, that would be nice, but not tonight Pete. I'm tired and a bit confused about things, so I'll be having an early night.'

'I could join you for that.'

'No, thanks for the tempting thought, but I'm bushed, call me tomorrow please.'

Chris finished getting Ivor's drink and passed it over as he said 'would you like to do a couple of 'lines'?'

'Ok, fine', she responded and went to fetch her bag of cocaine. They snorted together and she was feeling the effects almost immediately. She looked demurely at Ivor and slowly undid her blouse to reveal her full breasts and taut, aroused, nipples. He liked it when she played coy, she thought, and led him into the bedroom.

Ivor was not one for subtlety, tenderness or foreplay. He ripped off her skirt and panties and with no further delay used her mercilessly. As soon as he had finished, he rolled off her and fell into a dreamless sleep.

The next morning Ivor demanded sex again and she dutifully complied. A quick breakfast and he was off again to the airport for his flight to Auckland, before returning back to Rarotonga.

# CHAPTER 13

Pete dawdled over breakfast, not excited by another day in the office. 0830 had come and gone. As he got up his mobile rang: the Colonel.

'Morning Pete, it's Duncan. Just thought I should let you know they've decided to formally declare your brother missing next week. They will give Christine another fortnight to vacate the married quarter. Do you want to tell her or should I?'

'Thanks. I'll go around there now.'

Pete walked the kilometre or so to Christine's house with mixed feelings, some of those feelings being unmistakably guilt. He had regarded himself as a man of integrity and had spent some years mentally castigating his brother for betraying him, yet here he was readily embarking on an illicit relationship with his brother's wife. He was undoubtably still attracted to her but with her going South soon, what future was there in that. Besides, there was no denying her marriage to his brother. Could he, with any sense of honour, now betray Andy? Indeed, he thought, he had already done so and deserved his own damaged sense of self-worth. He was approaching the house quite slowly and saw someone just departing the place. Business type, he thought, rumpled grey suit. Why did that ring a bell? The man turned slightly toward him before heading down the street and Pete had a momentary mental blank before realizing he had seen that face before somewhere. Good grief, he thought with shock, it's the guy in the Sydney photos. He pulled out his phone, initially fumbled the keys, but eventually sorted out his contacts and rang Phil Stroud.

'Phil, it's Pete. That guy in the photos you showed me: I've just seen him. He's here!'

'Are you certain?' This was a fairly predictable immediate response and Pete didn't respond.

'Ok, I'm on to it', said Phil, 'do you still have him in sight?'

'Afraid not, he disappeared around the corner before I could get near him. I think he may have driven off because I still couldn't see him when I got to that corner.'

'There's not much we can do about it, but I'll pass the photos to the local police and see if they come up with anything.'

'Thanks Phil, catch you later', Pete was over his initial mix of surprise and confusion and continued on to Christine's.

The door was opened quite quickly after his first knock. Chris was still in her dressing gown, her hair still tousled, and stood there with a questioning look.

'Sorry to disturb so early', Pete started, 'although I see you have already had an early visitor.'

Chris looked nervously away toward the dining table and Pete noticed a bulky envelope lying there.

'Oh, that was just an over-eager real estate agent', Chris explained. 'I am looking into staying in Moresby for a while so will need a place to rent.'

'Right', Pete acknowledged, 'that's why I dropped around. I have just been told that Andy is going to be declared missing next week and I'm afraid that means you will need to vacate this place. They've offered you a couple of extra weeks to get organized. I suspect they will want your diplomatic passport too, at some stage.'

'No problem, I'll decide what I am going to do over the next few days', Chris responded. As she did so, her silk dressing gown drifted open and this made it quite clear that she had nothing else underneath. 'Meanwhile, I'm going back to bed', she smiled, although somewhat tiredly, 'want to join me?'

Pete was sorely tempted in a physical sense, but mentally there were alarm bells ringing and his conscience clamouring even more loudly. 'That sounds a wonderful option', he stuttered, 'but I really have to get back to the office. Maybe I could call you later?'

'You have a good day, Pete, call me any time.'

Pete walked away from the house with his emotions in turmoil. Chris was a liar, he thought, but why he had no idea. Equally, she had made it abundantly clear that she would be happy to continue their rekindled relationship. By the time he got back to the office he was no clearer on what he should do. There he was met by a bemused Angela who had a well-worn postal item in her hand.

'This has come "return to sender", she began, 'but oddly enough it was originally addressed to you', and she handed over the small packet.

Sure enough, the package was addressed to himself in Sydney and Andrew Martyn was listed as sender. The postmark was hard to read but he could just make out the RA and L of what could only be 'Rabaul'. Pete opened it with a mix of excitement and trepidation. There were two photographs, a phone SIM card and a sheet of rough notes in what he recognized as Andy's untidy handwriting. There was no covering letter nor any explanation for the contents. He looked closely at the photographs. One was of a sleek-looking ocean-going motor cruiser, the other a dark image in which he could make out what looked like an open box of rifles with what could be torchlight showing one of the serial numbers. The letters 'ST-K' were clearly stenciled on the side of the box. Pete shook his head in an attempt to clear his muddled mind and rang Phil Stroud.

'No joy yet on your man, Pete, but the locals have an eye out for him if he surfaces' advised Phil.

'Actually, it's not about that, I have a package here I think you should have a look at.'

'You in your office?' queried Phil and to the affirmative response said 'I'll be right along.'

Phil arrived in short order, took one look at the items spread out on Pete's desk and said 'I suppose you have smeared your fingerprints all over this stuff. Never mind, we'll sort that out.' He then extracted a pair of pale surgical gloves from his pocket and slowly separated the items out. He examined each item in turn and then ordered 'don't touch. I'll be back.'

He returned a few minutes later with a plastic evidence bag into which he popped the entire collection. 'We don't have much of a forensics capability here', he advised 'but I'll give this a good going over in my private dungeon and get back to you. The stuff will probably have to go to Canberra for a proper analysis.'

The day wore on tediously for Pete, with a low point reached when he asked Angela in for a chat and posed the question nagging his mind.

'Angela, it has been suggested to me that you might have been having a relationship with my brother. Is there any truth in that?'

Angela gave a loud guffaw off laughter and burst out 'well, there's only one place that piece of nonsense could have come from!' Then, more seriously, 'no Sir, I was definitely not having an affair with the Commander, nor any sort of relationship except routine office business.'

That settled Pete's mind about Angela, but at the same time disturbed him about why Chris would have accused her. His day then brightened with another visit from Phil Stroud.

'God I'm good', boasted the AFP agent, parking himself on the end of Pete's desk. The weapons are older 5.56mm SAR-21s from Singapore Technologies Kinetics, which explains the ST-K marking on the box. The Singaporeans have been especially helpful and the serial number that was visible is one of a batch of 30 sold to the Cook Islands police force about a year ago. They are pretty high-end weapons but have been superseded in Singapore and this was probably a second-hand batch from their army. Now the vessel. She is the 'Blue Turtle', a 75-foot Hatteras long-range motor cruiser registered in Rarotonga, Cook Islands, to a company called 'Pacific Gems'. See, I should have been a detective!' Phil finished with his usual dry sense of humour. 'There is a mixed bag of other shots on the SIM but mainly murky, all seem to have been taken in the dark. There is one shot of a chart with a single position marked 'DQ' a few hundred miles East of Fiji but I can't tell what that's about.

'So, we know Andy was in Rabaul, we know he was interested in a boat called Blue Turtle and we suspect that boat was shipping arms about', Pete summarized. 'It also seems vaguely possible that the Cook Islands may be involved in some way. It sounds equally possible, maybe even likely, that he got himself into something way over his head', he ventured.

'True enough, but it's not a lot to go on', added Phil. 'Let's see what the guys in Canberra come up with.'

'There is just one other thing, Andy, and it's scary. I am pretty certain that guy in the grey suit came out of Christine's house. Do you think she could be involved in some way, or possibly at risk?'

'Speculation Captain! The road to investigative ruin, they say. I'll keep my nose to the ground but for now I suggest you put those thoughts out of your mind.'

# CHAPTER 14

I could really get used to this, Andrew thought as he lay on the beach with Tamika, who had hardly left his side the whole time he had been here. If you set aside the violent and demeaning manner in which he had arrived here that is. The sun was shining in a cloudless pastel blue sky, gentle waves leapt gingerly over the outer ring of coral and the company was someone that men's dreams are made of. He thought back to what 'the Chief', as he now thought of him, had been saying. It made sense as far as it went. You would also need to set aside the business of gun-running and violent kidnapping, not minor demeanours by anyone's gauge, to consider them all a pretty cool bunch of people. Sure, Sopolo seemed tyrannical at first sight, and Tomas was certainly only one step removed from being the neighbourhood thug, but everyone else was relaxed, polite and exceptionally easy to get on with.

The Chief had introduced him to his new duties, little more than being a glorified school teacher really. There was a miscellany of ages amongst the younger generation on the island. The majority were apparently in their late teens but with a smattering of much younger children, well-spoken and mildly mannered. The island's challenge lay in its remoteness. Apparently, the occasional professional teacher arrived from the main island on the monthly barge but rarely stayed for long and most departed on the next available vessel. His aim was established as being to prepare the older kids so they could ultimately pass the university entrance exams in Australia, whilst no particular target was set for the younger ones. The weekly routine was explained as being daily school in the mornings six days a week, afternoons sport or free-time, and Sunday mornings compulsory church but no work. In many ways the local population seemed very conservative. That did not fully extend to physical relationships though, and sexual arrangements amongst the older teenagers seemed tacitly encouraged.

Time was becoming blurred, and this was fairly easy on the island. After what seemed like a couple of weeks of this easygoing life, Andy had settled into a routine and was starting to get to know the youngsters he was teaching, albeit in amateurish fashion. Their interests were such as one might find anywhere in the world but when queried about career aspirations the mix departed from his European-imbued expectations. There was no-one aiming to be pilot, lawyer, surgeon or engineer. Rather, their goals were down to earth and practical – business manager, teacher, policeman and, to his delight quite a few of the boys wanted to be seamen. That set his mind on the road to escape options, which clearly had to be somehow by sea.

'Tamika, when does the next barge come?

'End of month, next week I think', Tamika answered.

Andy rolled on to his side, stared into her deep brown eyes and asked 'Tamika, do you sleep with me because you want to or because you have to?'

Those brown eyes widened markedly and she said disarmingly 'I like you. It is enough.' Tamika had a broad vocabulary and was invariably well spoken but habitually spoke in short bursts. She smiled broadly and reached out to hold his hand.

'Tamika, I need to get off these pills', he stated, probably more forcefully than he intended. He had already noticed that, whilst full of vigour after his morning pill, he was increasing anxious and sweaty as the day wore on. He had actually started to look forward to his evening dose.

She snatched her hand back and looked closely back at him. 'No. You must take them. We both in big trouble if you stop. If Tomas find out he hurt us. Even worse when Ivor comes back.'

'Who is Ivor?' That simple question seemed to cause Tamika a great deal of distress.

'He very bad', she said bleakly, 'the Chief's bodyguard. He wants me but Chief not let him.'

Things were apparently going to be more challenging than he thought. If Tamika wouldn't help him, he needed to gather the strength to wean himself of this MDMA before it destroyed him. If this Ivor person was going to be an additional problem then it needed to be sooner rather than later. He let his mind wander back to his temporary students. The older teenagers were unremarkable in their behaviour and outlook he thought, but there was an odd group of youngsters. These were between about nine and twelve years old and just the five of them. They were a close-knit group and kept much to themselves. They were patently not as comfortable in their surroundings as the older group and had no obvious family connections.

'Where are the parents of the youngest of the students, Tamika?' He asked this innocently enough and added, 'I never see them around.'

There was a stronger reaction from Tamika than he expected. 'The parents live on the main island', she began, 'they are all important people and send their children here to be away from bad influences.'

'Do they get to see their parents often?'

'They have video calls every so often. Parents very busy people. Girls are daughters of Prime Minister and Deputy. Eldest boy's father is police chief.'

'Wow', Andy thought, those are pretty significant people. 'So, there are phones on the island?'

'Through satellite', Tamika responded. 'In Chief's office.'

Curiouser and curiouser cried Alice. Andy wasn't quite sure how that quote entered his head but it certainly summed up his current thoughts. What it did do was reinforce his determination to do something positive to resolve his position. There was some form of external communications in the Chief's office, he now knew, and there would certainly be some on any of the boats that came in. The mine, he thought, that must be able to communicate, at least back to Rarotonga. He determined to do something about it.

That evening he managed some sleight of hand to avoid swallowing the dreaded pill and that challenged him mentally much more than he anticipated. As night fell, he and Tamika made love in their usual gentle fashion and she drifted off to sleep. He feigned sleep himself for as long as he thought he could without dropping off himself and then quietly got up from the futon and slipped on some shorts. Tamika stirred dozily but did not waken. He crept carefully out of the hut and looked around. There was utter silence in all directions. He expected the darkness, but not the pitch black he encountered. Then he saw a faint flicker of light to his right which must have come from the village. Thus oriented, and knowing that Tamika's hut was at the end of the row, he turned left and started slowly along the crushed coral track that he believed led to the mine. He had gone no more than a hundred metres when he sensed someone next to him. He stopped and was pushed to the side of the track.

'You are foolish man' whispered Tamika.

'What are you doing here?' His question, short and simple as it was, took all his effort whilst trying to get over the shock of being discovered.

'I'm here because you're here', she stated simply. 'If you do this, then I try to keep you from getting hurt.'

'Do what?'

'Andrew, I am not stupid', she began quietly, 'I know things are not right on this island and if I can help make things better then I will. But you must know: there is much danger. You want to see mine, no?' Without waiting for an answer, she said 'come' and took his hand.

They variously walked and jogged for what must have been about three kilometres along the coral track winding through dense thickets and overhead coconut trees. He was slowly getting his night vision but realized he would have had no hope of making this trip on his own. What made matters worse was a realization that he was sweating, despite the cool evening, and subconsciously clenching his teeth, no doubt the result of withdrawal. As the sound of waves breaking on coral became louder, Tamika slowed to a halt and pointed. Ahead was a tall wire enclosure and the silhouette of two large huts could be seen. Tamika pulled him toward herself and whispered in his ear. 'Quiet, guard!'

In what little starlight that prevailed, he could see that there was a track to the left around the perimeter of the wire fence. Tamika led him that way. After about a hundred metres they were back on the soft sand of a beach. Following Tamika's lead, he started to walk in a slight crouch toward the fence where an old gap in the wire had obviously never been attended to. Inside the fence, and with his heart racing, Andy could just see the back of what must be the main building. There were small barred windows all along its side. Stretching to full height he could just see inside from where a pale light shone from an office doorway. He could see little else, but even that was suspicious enough: no mining machinery, no slag heaps outside, no gantries. All he could see were 44-gallon drums, smaller containers and chemistry apparatus of some sort littering a very large table. There were full polythene bags of varying sizes in the near corner.

'Come', Tamika's whisper seemed unusually loud in his tense state but he obeyed and followed her quietly back through the fence. The jog back to their hut was thankfully uneventful, although his feet hurt badly. Back in bed together, she simply put her finger to her lips, rolled over and promptly went back to sleep.

His thoughts were once again in turmoil. That there was no diamond mine he was almost positive. He could think up few options except drugs of some sort and his mind struggled to put the pieces of the jigsaw together before falling into a deep sleep. He was woken by an agitated Tamika, grabbing his feet. They were covered in blood.

'Quick, get dressed and come with me', she ordered, 'and make sure to wear sandals.'

Knocking on the door of the medical hut soon revealed a middle-aged buxom and motherly-looking woman who was the island's nurse practitioner. She soon had Andy sitting with his feet raised on a table as she tut-tutted at the blood and lacerations. 'Coral dust very risky', she said as she washed away the blood with fresh water. 'This may hurt', and she scoured the soles of his feet with an abrasive cloth and vinegar. 'Now you take some antibiotics', she added as she cleaned up 'are you allergic to anything?' A negative response elicited a packet of amoxicillin and the advice, forcefully put, to take three per day until finished. 'Coral infection can be very serious', the nurse added, 'you make sure you follow directions and don't go barefoot for a while.'

With that, the pair departed for their hut, only for Tamika to halt mid-stride and point out to sea. 'Here's trouble. Hemi's boat is coming in and probably has Ivor onboard.'

Regardless, they continued to their hut, being passed on the way by a tractor driven by Tomas towing a trailer and headed toward the wharf. For no obvious reason Tomas glowered at them both as he passed.

'They will have supplies onboard for the mine', Tamika explained as she fished out some band-aids to cover the worst of the lacerations on his feet. With all done, they headed off to the schoolroom.

Later that morning, with a slightly bored group of students taking it in turns to read from a biblical text, a European figure loomed at the door. 'You Martyn?' The question was probably superfluous as Andy was the only other European on the island as far as he knew. He nodded. Tamika whispered 'Ivor!'

'Out here!' Ivor ordered and pointed to Tamika, 'you too'.

Andy walked slowly out into the sunlight and was immediately and unexpectedly hit with a powerful punch to his solar plexus, with Ivor using all his considerable strength. Andy doubled over and came up short as a knee came up to connect with his jaw and he collapsed in a heap. Tamika screamed as Ivor laid into Andy's prone body with his feet.

'Help, help', Tamika screamed and this drew a small group of the male students out on to the track. These were not simply students; they were Islanders of considerable size and physique. They liked Tamika and had been quite taken with the friendly newcomer. Accordingly, they crowded around Andy's disabled figure and faced Ivor threateningly. There were many surrounding shouts of anger and alarm and a low growl from the youths as Ivor made a grab for Tamika. Movements came to a sudden halt, though, as a gunshot sounded close by and the Chief stalked forward with a pistol in his hand.

'What's going on here?' he shouted.

'This bastard has been nosing around the mine, that's what', yelled Ivor.

'And we know this because?' The Chief's question was tinged with doubt: he was coming to enjoy Andy's company.

'Tomas found blood on the track outside the front gate. Check his feet!'

There was little need to check. Andy's feet were clearly bloodied and the soles covered in band-aids.

'Secure him while I consider this', ordered the Chief, handing the pistol over to Ivor.

'Her too?' queried Ivor.

A nod from the Chief and Ivor positively glowed. He waved the pistol at Andy and gestured he and Tamika back along the track. They passed a hut marked 'Police' and Tomas stepped out.

'Grab a rifle and some cuffs' yelled Ivor.

That done, Andy and Tamika were prodded along the track toward the mine.

'Cuff them to the fence', directed Ivor. I've got to head out tomorrow to pick up the next shipment, so they're your responsibility. I'll get one of the crew to help but don't damage them. If you leave the chick alone you can have her when I get back - after I've finished with her that is. With that he returned to the village leaving a sorry pair of bedraggled prisoners virtually helpless.

# CHAPTER 15

In a large building not far from the Attorney-General's Department in Canberra, and technically subordinate to it, is the Federal Police headquarters. Amongst a miscellany of offices is a large operations room that doubles as a video conferencing facility. On this particular day there were few officers occupying the room, three of whom were Agent Garry Walsh, a Customs officer from Border Force and a Navy liaison officer. They were collectively addressing what was becoming known internally as the Cook Islands issue. There were additionally two remote participants on video, Sergeant Johansson of the NSW Police and Agent Stroud from Port Moresby.

'If you guys don't mind. I'll take the lead on this', began Agent Walsh, 'although to be frank I'm not sure how any of this jig-saw fits together, if at all. Here's what we know, or think we know, so far. We have had the house of a Navy Commander blown up, killing his wife, at about the same time as his brother, another Navy Commander, goes missing from Port Moresby. There is photographic evidence of a boat registered in the Cook Islands carrying arms, destination unknown, except we know that it called at Rabaul, possibly on the way home. We also know that the Cook Islands' government has put a no-go zone around one of their islands, supposedly to protect a diamond mine that may or may not exist. Equally, and this is what concerns our NZ brethren, they have called a halt to fisheries surveillance flights in the area. OK, Guys, what else?'

Sergeant Johansson the chipped in. 'We have a confirmed ID on the man in the grey suit seen near the scene of the explosion and also with the hooker the same day. He is a New Zealand national, Cook Islands resident, named Ivor Slavinski. Thank you to our Border Force colleagues who confirmed the ID from passport details on his departure from Darwin airport a few days later. We have no real idea how he got to Darwin but domestic flights don't need passports and he may well have used an alias. We have also done a thorough check of retail counter camera records of the shops where Andrew Martyn's credit card was used. I can now confirm that those purchases were actually made by Slavinski.'

'I can add a bit to that', commented Phil Stroud, 'we had him eyeballed in Port Moresby a couple of days ago and flight checks showed him returning via Darwin from Hong Kong and then leaving for Auckland and Rarotonga. He's been a busy boy but what he's been up to we really don't know! There may be some connection with Christine Martyn, Andrew's wife, but that's unconfirmed. I have the local PNG people keeping a weather eye on her.'

'Can we put an Interpol Red Note out on Slavinski?' This question from Sergeant Johansson drew a quick negative from the Canberra AFP man. 'We simply don't have enough I'm afraid. We have strong suspicions about involvement in the explosion and also the assault in Sydney, but not enough for charges yet, and certainly not enough for an Interpol warrant or extradition request.'

'So how does the Da Qing figure in all this', asked the Customs woman. 'We have bits and pieces of information but I don't see how they fit with your own investigation. 'Although', she added after a short pause as something triggered a memory 'when was Slavinski in Hong Kong?'

'Wednesday last according to the Chinese', Garry replied.

Some shuffling of papers, and then the Customs representative continued 'well, it may be a coincidence, but that was when Da Qing was in Hong Kong. Her destination is listed as Sydney via Auckland. But', she emphasized, 'I can assure you that she has not been landing contraband at either port on previous trips because we went through that ship with a fine tooth-comb. I know that you have previously advised us of the Chinese concerns but they are a bit vague and not really anything for us to go on.'

Garry looked apologetic and said, somewhat abashed, 'sorry, we have had a bit of clarity from them on that score. Apparently, the issue that has attracted their attention is a flow of what could be pre-cursor chemicals from a warehouse in Shanghai on to the Da Qing.'

'Suspicions, suspicions', remarked the Customs lady, 'I need something a bit more concrete to go on before I start putting extra resources on this.'

'Maybe I can add something', interjected the Defence officer 'at the AFP's request we put Da Qing on our watch list. She was picked up a few days out of Hong Kong by a surveillance P3. Apparently, she has switched off her AIS - the ship tracking system - but if she keeps on her present course she will end up East of Fiji.'

This comment triggered an immediate reaction from Phil Stroud. 'That triggers a memory. Can you guys give me a couple of minutes while I go check?' Without waiting for a response, Phil grabbed his photographs from the Blue Turtle and raced up to Pete Martyn's office.

'Pete', he said as he burst into his office 'would you be able to give me a Lat and Long on this DQ marking on this photo?'

Pete looked up and took the photograph. 'I need to see some edges of the chart concerned to be accurate, but I suppose I could work it out. When do you want it?'

'Yesterday, if not sooner', Phil said, 'it could be the breakthrough we need and Canberra is waiting for it right now.'

Pete grabbed a South Pacific chart from a side-table and spread it in front of him, pulling out a pair of dividers from his drawer. After about a minute of calculation he wrote down some figures on note paper and said 'there you go, close enough I think, certainly within a couple of miles.'

Phil almost yelled his thanks as he departed the office in a rush. Back in his own space and with video still streaming, he caught the end of some comments from the Defence officer. 'Switching off AIS is not legitimate but she's outside our jurisdiction and it's a matter for the civil maritime people anyway.'

'Ok, I see Phil is back with us. What do you have Phil?'

'Thanks Garry', Phil began, 'the comment about Da Qing going East of Fiji reminded me of that 'DQ' marking on the photographs from the Cook Islands vessel. That marking is a few hundred miles East of Fiji. I have the exact coordinates here. Could that be a rendezvous, do you think?'

'Makes sense', commented Garry, 'what do you guys think?'

'Let me recap a moment please', was the Customs officer's response. 'We have Chinese suspicions of possible', she emphasized the word, 'precursor chemicals on this Da Qing. We know that she has not been offloading in her destination ports of Auckland or Sydney so where are they going? What is East of Fiji?'

The Defence and AFP officers called almost in unison 'the Cook Islands.'

There was moment's silence as they all absorbed this information.

'God, we need an asset of some sort up there', commented Garry, 'any ideas?' His question was directed initially at the Defence officer who looked somewhat doubtful.

'We could put a ship in the area, but it would get there far too late for any meaningful involvement, and we certainly can't board a vessel on the high seas. Maybe we could task a P3 to keep an eye on that location around the time Da Qing is due to get there but I would need some formal request from one of your people.'

'Consider it done' replied Garry, 'I'll ask the boss.'

'What about someone on the ground over there?' This query from Phil who had just the right person in mind.

'Risky', said Garry. 'I suspect you are thinking of the brother?' This with a questioning lift of the eyebrows.

'Yes, it could be useful if we can put together a plausible reason. I suppose he would have to agree, as I concur in the risk.'

'There is a donated patrol boat out there provided under the government's Pacific Patrol Boat program', offered the Defence officer. 'We could ask for a progress check on their degree of satisfaction perhaps.'

'Ok', murmured Garry, let's do that as well and see where this gets us. We really haven't addressed the diamonds issue but that can wait until this element gets sorted.'

Each member of the meeting nodded, grateful to be allowed out for a delayed lunch, and went their separate ways.

# CHAPTER 16

There were serious looks on both sides of the desk as Phil
Stroud was briefing Pete Martyn on what they knew of the disparate but equally suspicious links they had uncovered regarding the Cook Islands.

'We are going to ask you to go there and have a nose around',
Phil was saying, 'but there is an undefinable risk and no compul-
sion.'

'I can't see what this possibly has to do with my brother, Phil,
but I would be happy to go, just to get some breathing space distant from here. I do believe, anyway, that falls within my role as
we, that is the Defence staff, do have 'watching brief' responsibility for South Pacific countries.

'Good man', said Phil. 'You should get some sort of marching
orders pretty soon, but I'm not sure where from.'

'Thanks Phil, I'll let you know what, if anything, comes
through. Before you go, is there anything new on my sister-in-
law?'

'Nothing I can tell you right now, sorry, but if I were you, I
would give her a wide berth for a while, at least until you get
back.'

Pete mulled over this for a while and decided he had better let
Angela know what was planned. Before he could do that, his mobile rang: his uncle. 'Yes, Sir.'

'Peter, we have had a request from Canberra for a visit to
see how the Cook Islanders are getting on with their new patrol boat', began the Maritime Commander, 'and you seem best
placed to do that. Any issues you can pass straight to this headquarters before bothering Canberra, if you get my drift. You

have my number, call if you need anything.'

Pete rang off and called Angela in. 'Can you get me flights to Rarotonga please, as soon as that's possible? Is there any way I can get a government credit card to cover costs?'

Angela was as efficient as ever and came back within the hour. 'I can get you on a flight from Brisbane to Rarotonga day after to-morrow, but you will have to get the red-eye via Darwin tonight and another overnight in Fiji. Next available flight is from Sydney via Auckland but that doesn't leave for another four days. Credit card is possible but it will take a week to organize as the Colonel needs authorization from Canberra.'

'Thanks Angela, well done. I'll go tonight. Can you fix that up while I go back to the hotel and get packed? Forget the credit card, I'll sort something out over there.'

Two days later Pete was checking in at a hotel in Muri Beach, Rarotonga thinking firstly that Angela had good taste and secondly that he probably couldn't afford this place. His needs, apart from never seeing another airport for a very long time, extended little further than an ice-cold beer and a visit to the gym. Unpacked and deciding to forgo the beer, he headed to the gym and began to exorcise his demons on a treadmill. The only other occupant was a very attractive Asian-looking woman lifting weights, which seemed at odds with her apparently slight and delicate appearance. His ego rose encouragingly as his admiring glances seemed to be frequently returned.

A long shower later and a check of his very limited wardrobe left Pete sitting on his bed in open-neck shirt and slacks whilst staring at his thin wallet. He had perhaps $200 in cash and a maxed-out credit card. That was not going to cover getting around town, let alone getting across to the other end of the islands. He reached for the phone to call his uncle but thought better of it. As he did so, he noticed a forgotten business card in his wallet – 'Samuel Goldman, Financier'. Doubts cast aside, he rang.

'Mr Goldman, you may not remember me but you attended my wife's funeral', he began haltingly, 'my name is Peter Martyn and

I find myself in a bit of a temporary financial pickle. As I see from your card that you are a financier, I wondered whether you might be able to arrange some credit?'

'Ah, the good Commander', Goldman responded, 'I remember you well for looking after my son and would be happy to help you, although credit is not the usual sort of financing I do. How much do you need?'

'Around $10,000 should cover me until I can get reimbursed back in Port Moresby', Pete answered, wondering if this was just going to be an embarrassing and fruitless request.

'Give me the name of your bank', was the short demand.

Pete had to think fast. 'Well, I am an ANZ customer but I'm in the Cook Islands at the moment, Rarotonga.'

'It is my experienced view that honest people never ask for as much as they will really need', avowed Goldman, 'there will be $20,000 sitting in your name in the ANZ bank in Rarotonga by start of business tomorrow. You may repay me anytime, but I insist that you visit me when next in Sydney so we can see if the money was well spent.'

To say that Pete was astonished was a mild understatement. He headed out from the hotel in high spirits and took a cab to what his driver declared to be the largest and finest jewelry store in Rarotonga. He stepped inside to a smorgasbord of fine jewelry and noticed, as he wandered around the counters that the Asian woman from the hotel gym was also there admiring a fine pair of pearl ear-rings. Looking at the attentive assistant he paused and said 'actually, I was looking for diamonds', and was somewhat doubtful about the likely reaction.

'I'm sorry sir, we don't sell diamonds', said the apologetic assistant. A lady who was perhaps the store manager came across and interrupted. 'Actually, we do have a few that came in last week on consignment, but they are as yet uncut and unpolished', she advised. 'What exactly were you looking for?'

Pete had not rehearsed this problem and was out of his depth. 'Er, well', he started, 'I don't have time to get anything cut while I'm here, perhaps something I could get cut at home to my own specifications.'

The manager looked at him with a slightly superior smile and said 'let me show you something and see what you think'. She placed a black felt pad in front of him on which she placed a cubic-looking object. He examined it knowing he had no idea of what to look for: it just looked like a piece of faintly yellowish rock to him.

'Maybe I could help?' The Asian lady was apparently aspiring to be a good Samaritan. 'Could I borrow your glass please?' she asked the manager in perfectly modulated Oxford English.

The unknown woman then examined the piece carefully and advised 'it could be cut in a variety of ways, but the colour will not be first-rate and you will be taking a chance on the clarity. I also suspect it has a flaw, but you won't know that for certain until it's cut. I would guess this is about two carats. How much?' she finished.

'I could let you have that for four hundred dollars.' Answered the manager promptly.

'Fair price', said is new-found helper, who then looked at him enquiringly.

Was that a discreet nod he asked himself. Surely not, but for reasons entirely unclear to himself he decided 'OK, I'll take it, but not right now, I'll collect it tomorrow.'

Outside the store he turned to the Asian lady, perhaps Chinese he wondered, to thank her for her help but she had already disappeared down the street. Instead he asked for directions to the wharf and proceeded as advised. It was a long walk, but in the fresh early summer air was not unpleasant. At the wharf the silhouette of the 40-metre Guardian Class patrol boat was unmistakable. He introduced himself to the sailor at the gangway who went away and returned with a smartly-uniformed officer wearing four gold stripes on his shoulders.

'Captain Martyn, welcome aboard', he said smiling, 'I'm Jacob. We received a message from your Navy HQ telling us to expect you. Would you like a look around?'

To his affirmative response the skipper waved across a young officer from nearby and gave him relevant instructions.

'I have some paperwork to finish off, but when you are finished come up to my cabin for a coffee', finished the skipper.

Pete was shown around the vessel in accommodating and professional manner and finished up in the captain's cabin.

'She is certainly a magnificent vessel, skipper', he began, 'the main question is are you happy with her?'

The skipper waited until some coffee arrived, then proceeded to canvas almost every feature of his ship with comment, positive or less so, on each. There was obvious pride in the ship and her crew and they were soon chatting like fellow professionals. At what he thought might be a suitable moment Pete casually asked 'what do you know about Rakahanga Island?'

Jacob frowned, 'not allowed to go there now', he said, 'that place is a pretty touchy subject in high places and, if I were you, I would be careful asking questions about the place.'

'Oh, I only asked as I heard the Kiwis were worried about not being allowed to fly their P-3 flights around the area.'

'I can't comment on that', Jacob replied, 'but I am under strict instructions from the Police Chief, who I work for, to stay clear of the place.'

Pete left the ship on friendly terms and headed by cab back to the hotel, where he went directly to the bar and sat quietly thinking over a cold beer.

'Mind if I join you?' A burly man in T-shirt and shorts sat down at his table without waiting for a response. 'I'm escaping', he asserted, 'name's Charlie. Got a boat down the harbour and headed for Fiji tomorrow but need a break from the Missus.' He sat and plonked his own schooner of beer on the table. 'Love sailing, but cooped up with the Missus for weeks on end can be a bit wearing. With luck, we should just get back to Wellington before killing each other', he finished in a strong Kiwi accent.

Pete's antennae were at full stretch. 'What sort of a boat do you have?' he asked innocently.

'Sailing cat, Leopard 45, she's a South African job, not so new anymore but a real beauty in a decent wind', Charlie expounded.

'Done any sailing yourself?'

'Actually, I have done quite a bit of yachting in my time', Pete replied, 'can I get you another beer?'

'Gentlemanly of you, I'm sure', Charlie happily agreed.

Returning from the bar and sipping his beer quietly, Pete asked the key question that was burning him up. 'Don't suppose you'd take a temporary crew member for a couple of days?'

Charlie looked at him curiously. 'We are not stopping anywhere until Fiji, where did you want to go?'

'Could you maybe drop me off on the way near one of the northern islands?' Pete ventured. 'I could get an inflatable so you wouldn't have to stop.'

'That's not exactly on our way', Charlie responded, 'in fact it's a few hundred miles north. So why don't you tell me exactly what you're after?'

Pete was stuck. He either spun an unlikely yarn or told Charlie the truth. He certainly wasn't going to cooperate otherwise. He edged his chair a little closer and lowered his voice. "I'm a Naval officer', he began, 'the NZ government have been prevented from undergoing their usual surveillance of the northern islands and I have been asked to find out why.' He watched to see Charlie's reaction and realized that he was holding his breath.

'Got any ID?' was Charlie's response.

'OK, come with me', was all that was said after Pete's ID was checked.

They went together down to the boat harbour and onboard Charlie's large, good-looking catamaran berthed alongside.

'Maryanne', he called and a bright-eyed woman in her fifties came out of the main cabin. 'This here's Pete', Charlie explained. 'He seems kosher and wants a lift up to the northern islands. What do you think?'

'We are in no rush, Charlie, so if you think it's ok, then it's ok by me.'

Pete let out a sigh of relief as Charlie said 'you'd best get on with arranging the dinghy and stuff, and a bit of extra tucker wouldn't go astray. Don't spend too long, I want to be away before dark tomorrow.'

Pete wasted no time finding the local chandlery and organizing a small inflatable dinghy, air pump and outboard motor for pick-up the next day. Realizing he was entering unknown territory, he added as an afterthought, 'got any flare guns?' He was supplied with a one-inch flare gun and associated distress flares with the seller's cautionary 'don't forget you will have to register that.'

Hurriedly packed and checked out the next morning, he headed for the local ANZ Bank branch and presented his identity documents. He was greeted warmly and asked how he wanted the $20,000 sitting there in his name. He took $5,000 cash and put the rest on his credit card. Next stop the electronics shop for a satellite phone. He was pleasantly surprised to see his attractive lady friend there also. She looked around as he entered and smiled. 'I just need a new charger for my phone', she explained, 'what's your excuse?'

'Well, I would like to say that I came simply to thank you for your kind gesture yesterday, but really I need a complete new phone. I would, though, really like to thank you for rescuing me, I know little about diamonds. I'm Peter Martyn' he added.

'Pleased to meet you Mr Martyn, I'm Alison.'

She responded to his raised eyebrows and look of mild surprise. 'What's up Peter Martyn, can't a Chinese lady have a European name?'

'Touché! It's a lovely name Alison, but I'm in a bit of a rush and need a Sat phone. I don't suppose you know about them too?'

'Actually, I do', she retorted with another bright smile. 'I prefer Hawei, but they don't have them here. You could get a neat Iridium perhaps. I think they have a model here that's really quite compact and should set you back a bit over two thousand with a pre-paid plan.' She was a veritable mine of information and sure enough they had the model she suggested. He said polite goodbyes and departed hurriedly to pay for his diamond, new boat and associated gear. There was one short break on the way at a park bench where he set his phone to work and dialled an overseas number.

'Christ Pete', Arno swore, 'do you have any idea what time it is?'

'Sorry Arno but it's urgent. If I get you a raw diamond would you be able to tell where it came from?'

'Not myself, but one of the team probably could', he said sleepily 'mail it registered express and I'll get it looked at.'

'Thanks Arno.' Pete finished and headed back to the chandlery, paid out another $50 to get his purchases delivered to the boat harbour and headed for the post office.

By the time the sun was closing rapidly on the horizon Pete was hauling on a sheet with the Cat's sails pulling strongly and heading North.

# CHAPTER 17

Alison Ho watched the tall good-looking guy with the Australian accent leave the electronics shop and followed cautiously. She was suspicious of him and mentally started adding up the pieces of the puzzle. After monitoring his final purchases and his odd diversion to the post office she watched from a distance as he boarded a large sailing catamaran. She picked up her cellphone.

'We have some possible interference', she spoke into the phone and switched to Mandarin. 'Find out what you can on an Australian named Peter Martyn and I want to know where a sailing boat called 'Maryanne' is headed. Get me an airplane for Manihiki and pay whatever it costs to delay the barge to Rakahanga then get me on it. I want my travelling kit put together and left for me at the Muri Beach Hotel.'

Alison turned back toward her hotel and thought of jogging there until she realized that she was wearing high heels. Still, another session in the gym would make up for that. She probably didn't need it; she was a naturally very fit and healthy woman who tended to turn men's heads as she walked by. She settled down for a quiet night and waited for her contact to return her call. That happened in the early evening and, after reporting that he had been partly successful, he would report to the hotel at breakfast the next day.

Breakfast in the hotel was obviously a social occasion with the dining areas full of holiday-makers. Finally, she found an empty corner and settled down to a light breakfast. She was joined by an ascetic-looking older man with Asiatic features who sat quietly beside her, put down the kit-bag he was carrying and waved to an attendant for a cup of coffee. He spoke in Mandarin. 'Martyn is a Navy man who works at the Australian High Commission in Port Moresby. No record, but recent press reports are of an explosion in Sydney which killed his wife and the PNG Police had a watching brief on him. That's all on him. The Maryanne is a sailing yacht registered in Wellington to a local businessman named Charles Winston. The yacht is logged as sailing for Wellington via Fiji. That's all the intel I have for now. We can't get you on a commercial flight for six days. Your plane will be ready tomorrow. It has taken some time to get a suitable aircraft and it has had to be fitted with extended range fuel tanks to make sure it can return safely. It will be at the general aviation section of the airport at ten hundred tomorrow. Your pilot's name is Wenzhou and he is clean. The barge has been a very expensive problem. It is due to sail for Rakahanga tomorrow and is already running late. It's fixed but you will need to be careful with the skipper who is supposed to be on the take and handy with a knife. That's it: best of luck'. The visitor left without offering to pay for his coffee.

Alison finished her breakfast and contemplated what to do with the rest of her day. Dammit, she thought, I'm a free woman, I'll enjoy my otherwise wasted day. She wandered through the streets taking occasional photographs, detoured through a shopping mall and eventually on to the beach where she kicked off her shoes and enjoyed the simple pleasure of a paddle in the ocean. Back at the hotel a slowly sipped gin and tonic and an even more slowly eaten dinner and off to bed feeling like her job wasn't always so arduous. Nervous energy returned the next morning as she departed for the airport and made contact with her pilot. She was in no mood for socializing as the twin Cessna took to the air and apparently neither was the pilot. They maintained a cool silence throughout the flight until on final approach to the modern-looking airstrip at the NE corner of the island the pilot motioned her to tighten her seatbelt and advised 'there should be someone from the barge to pick you up. Don't know who but they can't miss the fact that we are about to arrive.'

On the ground in Manihiki an old Jeep trundled from a nearby hangar and up to the plane. The driver looked decidedly put out when he saw his prospective passenger.

'You Ho?' He almost spat the question. To her nod he added, 'they didn't tell me it was a woman.'

'Is that a problem?' queried Alison.

'Could be', the ragged-looking Islander responded, 'ain't got no facilities for women'. With that he gestured for her to get in the Jeep and off they clattered to the wharf.

There was no mistaking the barge they were about to embark on, which was actually an old army landing craft drawn up on the beach. It also became clear that her driver was also the barge skipper.

'I'm already late leaving, so get your gear stowed and stay out of the way', was the skipper's only further acknowledgement of her presence. They sailed almost immediately.

Alison was conscious that she was attracting plenty of admiring looks from the skipper and his two-man crew. Her choice of tight jeans and a tank top which served to emphasize her full breasts and slim waist was not helping. She threw a black floppy jumper on to disguise her figure a little and prepared herself for a vigilant night. To help these guys get the message she pulled a wicked-looking bayonet from her bag and began to make a point of sharpening it slowly and obviously. As it transpired, she had a peaceful if rather restless night sleeping on deck. Her tension levels began to rise again as they approached Rakahanga. She had no real plan of action and was going to have to make this up as she went along.

'When we berth you had better stay out of sight', ordered the barge skipper, 'they haven't been taking too kindly to strangers here lately, and I value my health.'

'Maybe you could just say I'm your new girlfriend', Alison suggested, 'I'll even give you a hug or two if it helps.'

That drew something between a smile and a scowl but seemed to mollify the skipper for the time being. Alison decided not to push her luck, though, and disappeared into a small compartment away from the cargo area. That didn't stop her hearing the yells from the wharf though, beginning with: 'you're bloody late as hell, you sonofabitch, I needed that diesel yesterday.' This in a very angry European voice. Alison decided to keep her low profile for a while and watched as they offloaded. The first items were a dozen drums of diesel, four of which went straight on to a sleek motor yacht berthed ahead of them. There was no rush to offload the rest of the stores which, as far as she could see, were innocent provisions of a kind to be expected for a remote island. The cruiser itself departed almost immediately.

'I want another two diesel drums up to the mine site', Alison heard as the cruiser left the wharf, and she started paying more attention. Two drums already on the wharf were set aside and as the afternoon wore on a tractor and trailer appeared, loaded the drums and disappeared up the beaten track through the village. She decided to wait until dark and settled down in her snug compartment, sorting her bag of gear and changing into an unbelievably figure-hugging black track suit and sneakers. After a quick visit to the wheelhouse she slipped quietly out onto the deck as night fell. There were lights and music in many buildings but no-one visible outside. Momentarily distracted by the carpet of a myriad stars above her and a sliver of a moon, she took a deep breath and headed ashore and up through the village.

# CHAPTER 18

Pete Martyn was getting his sea-legs back and quite enjoying the brisk motion of the 'Maryanne', named after the owner's new wife. She, the wife that is, was a good twenty years his junior and loved talking, so much so that Pete began to feel a degree of sympathy for Charlie. Still, he thought, you make your bed, you lie in it, and there were obvious compensations. Maryanne was a beautiful young woman! They were making good speed in a brisk Easterly wind and both the catamaran and her owner were reveling in the conditions. They had cleared the Southern Group of islands the morning after departure and then had a clear ocean run North toward Rakahanga. This was Pete's admitted destination and Charlie had cheerfully announced 'no problem!'

Pete had been keeping night watches to give Charlie a break, but that was very undemanding in the open waters on autopilot. As they approached nearer their destination Pete's nerves became a little more strained and he occupied himself getting his gear and dinghy ready for launching.

'I don't want to get too close to the island in daylight', Pete mentioned, 'but I do have a problem with the noise of the outboard at night. They would hear that from miles away with the wind in this onshore direction.'

'We could drop you off the West coast if that helps', offered Charlie, 'the main entry to the lagoon plus the wharf area are both that side too. Looking at the weather chart, though, things may look very different this time tomorrow evening.' Pete automatically looked skywards and noticed that the white clouds were becoming greyer and he realized that the boat was pitching more than previously. They pored over the weather chart on Charlie's computer together and came to the same conclusion. They were in for a north-westerly change with poor weather ahead. Only poor by the beneficent standards they had been enjoying though: stronger winds and probably some rain. They decided upon a landing somewhere on the South-Eastern coast.

Charlie and Maryanne both helped, despite the ungodly time of the morning: 3 AM. The dinghy was fully prepared and launched, attached with a line to the catamaran's stern, and Maryanne had put together a small pack of food with a couple of bottles of fresh water. Pete changed into the best he could manage as a landing outfit, merely jeans, dark shirt and a pair of soft leather boots he had acquired in Rarotonga. His nerves were definitely on edge as he was well aware that he had become unaccustomed to physical endeavours. Warm farewells followed, together with faint promises to meet up over a glass or two in Wellington, and Pete was on his way.

The catamaran sailed off without a sound, which was hardly what could be said for the outboard. It sounded raucous in comparison with the gentle beat of sheets and sails he had been getting used to. He worried that it could be heard from afar but kept the revs low and hoped that the increasing wind would muffle the noise of his approach. He could see almost nothing except the low silhouette of the island ahead and his tension levels increased yet again. Soon, and not far away, he could hear the gentle breaking of waves on the coral reef and headed for a darker patch he guessed as being the opening they had earlier decided on. Just then the patter of raindrops added to his discomfort whilst ahead he could now see the reef itself. He eased back on the throttle and let the dinghy's momentum carry it slowly forward. The bottom scraped noisily and he cut the throttle at the same time as the boat lurched upwards and slammed down. He had misjudged his speed and, feeling water spreading around his ankles, soon realized also that he had holed the boat.

There was little choice but to abandon the dinghy which was slowly tearing itself apart on the reef. He found himself standing in shallow water over the reef, but moved carefully on the rough underwater coral in fear of breaking an ankle. That would certainly bring a rapid halt to his mission he thought. Moving forward, he soon sank into chest deep water and tried to keep his back-pack, well-wrapped in plastic though it was, above the surface. He stumbled forward more than walked and with mental visions of sharks or alligators clouding his mind he had a momentary relief as he felt the ground rising and he was soon on sand. His next task was to orient himself, not so easy in the dark with rain now falling steadily. He knew that there was a shallow opening to the reef which he had obviously missed. If that was to his left, he would soon encounter it, if not then he was on the correct part of the island chain. He stumbled forward, squelching with every step, feeling miserable but determined.

He kept to the sand and was finding it hard going. His calf muscles were burning after only a few minutes but there were no clear openings off the beach, just a black wall of Pandanus and overhanging palm trees. He guessed he had gone about a kilometre when he thought he saw his first opening above the beach. Pulling out his torch and ripping off the heavy plastic wrapping, he risked a light toward the trees. Sure enough there was an opening off the beach. Not only that, there was evidently a vehicle track of some kind. He ventured up the track and after what seemed an interminable time, but was really only a few minutes, he saw the outline of buildings ahead. He needed to get much closer to assess whether this was his goal but realized the risk and trod exceptionally carefully. He came up to edge of a high chain-wire fence which the road continued alongside and veered left around what he thought could be the back of the buildings. He walked close to the fence and registered a small gap but went past.

Fifty metres on he came to a corner, still treading carefully on the rough ground. It remained hard to see in the drizzle, although he noted a glimmer of light from one of the buildings.

Security perhaps, he thought, although he was surprised that he had still come across no features he would have expected for a mine-site. Another forty metres and he was evidently at the front of the compound and he turned the corner with increasing confidence. That lasted only a few more metres when he was able to distinguish two figures next to the fence close to what must be the main gate. They were not moving and didn't seem to be conversing. He crept forward and knelt to watch. He was still on his knees when a cold steel something pressed into the side of his head.

'Stay very still, punk, and tell me who you are and what the hell you're doing here?' Tomas kept his rifle firmly against Pete's head and was seconds away from pulling the trigger.

With no time to think, Pete flopped onto one arm and looked up at his captor. 'I need help', he pleaded trying to look at least like a facsimile of a stranded sailor. 'Our boat sank off the coast during the night', he looked upwards. That was a mistake. The next moment he was covered in blood and gore and his mind froze. His captor also was frozen, but in his case with an arrow sticking through his skull. His expression was not visible but would doubtless have been a picture of surprise as he crumpled slowly to the ground. Out of the easing rain loomed a figure in a black skin-tight outfit carrying what looked like a miniature steel crossbow. Rather than give him aid to rise, though, his rescuer knelt and placed a wicked-looking and very sharp dagger to his throat.

'So, tell me, Peter Martyn, what's a Navy man from Port Moresby doing here on Rakahanga? No BS or your throat will gain a new breathing hole.'

'Good grief, Alison?' He recognized the dulcet Oxford tones although they seemed a little harsher than he recalled.

'Answer the question', Alison demanded fiercely, 'I've been sitting watching this compound all bloody night and I'm in no mood for messing around.'

'My government don't believe the diamond story and sent me to find out what's going on.'

'Pick the rifle up, stand up and keep me covered', Alison wasted no time in further discussion and knelt next to Tomas' body and started digging out the crossbow bolt with her knife. This was a messy business and Pete gagged. Alison looked up, seemed to shrug and said simply 'I only have two: waste not, want not.'

Standing together, they both looked toward the figures leaning against the fence near the main gate. They presented no obvious threat but both Pete and Alison moved slowly forward, rifle at the ready and crossbow reloaded. There was now a hint of twilight showing through the trees. Nonetheless, they were only a few metres away when Pete gave a surprised gasp and rushed towards the pair.

'Andrew!' That was all he managed before he saw that Andy was in no fit state to respond. His jaw was the size of a tennis ball and he was hanging by one arm from the fence. He lifted him to take the weight off his arm and hugged him tightly.

'Not so tight', was the hoarse whisper that Andy managed, 'broken ribs!'

My God, what a mess Pete thought as he looked at the girl next to his brother. She was in better shape but clearly at the limit of her strength and distraught. He looked at the handcuffs and struggled with what to do to free the prisoners. He looked behind him to Alison, 'my brother', he announced.

'Oh goodie, family amateur hour', Alison was caustic. It would have been pointless to argue, though, as she was clearly the most professional amongst them at this sort of thing. She proved this by extracting a slim metal object from her hairband then proceeding to unpick the handcuffs on the two prisoners.

'That'll be enough of that', called a voice from the gate. They stopped, particularly as the voice belonged to someone pointing another rifle at them. There was a flicker of movement from Alison and the unknown guard's rifle flew into the air as Alison's knife appeared firmly embedded in his neck. She ignored the fallen guard and concentrated on finishing unpicking the handcuffs. This she achieved as both prisoners fell to their knees, patently exhausted.

Pete stared at Alison. 'Who ARE you?' he asked.

Alison stared back at him. 'Detective-Inspector Alison Ho, Hong Kong Police.'

'Wow.' That was the limit of Pete's intellectual offering. Alison took charge. 'I think we had better take a look inside, don't you?' she offered and headed in through the open gates.

# CHAPTER 19

The interior of the building was cavernous but even with the increasing daylight it was still too dim to make out any significant detail of the contents. A pallid light came through the open door of a side office but on examination proved to be from a 12-volt emergency lantern.

'Generator?' This from Alison.

'I'll go look next door', offered Pete and he trudged next door to the smaller building. There a large generator sat proudly in the centre and any operating difficulties were solved by a well-labelled control panel on its front. The generator started with a roar on first attempt and lights came on from all directions.

'What's going on?' A short weaselly looking man came out of a back room rubbing sleep from his eyes.

Pete wasted neither time nor words, 'come with me' he ordered and shepherded the man into the main building. The man, who looked worn and bedraggled in dirty jeans and a sweat-shirt made no complaint about being so rudely awakened and simply followed Pete's direction. He did come to a stop when he saw the others inside the main building and looked confused.

'Why are you here? He questioned, 'don't touch anything, dangerous chemicals.'

'Are you the chemist?' Pete asked this from pure guesswork but received a positive nod from the man, whose named turned out to be Luis from Mexico. Pete looked over at Alison and added 'I need some rope.'

The walking multi-tool package that was Alison produced a set of cable ties from her back-pack and Pete proceeded to secure Luis' arms behind him. 'You are under arrest until we find out exactly what you have been up to here', Pete added, both superfluously and illegitimately. 'Stand over in the corner where we can see you.'

The room was an Aladdin's cave of chemical products, glassware of various sizes, retorts and clear plastic bags by the thousand. All this was neatly arranged around two central tables which appeared to be the focus of activities.

'Pseudoephedrine, Acetone, Toluene, Hydrochloric acid, Alison was reading drum labels aloud as she walked around the tables. 'Meth', 'Chalk' and 'Adam' were various printed labels in small piles.

'They're making Methylenedioxymethamphetamine and Methamphetamine – MDMA and Crystal Ice to you guys', Alison announced, 'this is about the largest drug lab I have ever come across. Take photos of everything', she directed as she pulled out a tiny camera and started photographing everything in sight. Having completed a full circuit, she plugged the camera into her sat phone, dialled some numbers and started speaking quickly in Mandarin. Meanwhile Pete had taken quite a few shots with his own phone and now dialled his uncle.

'It's Peter, Sir, he began. 'I'm at the place we spoke of and it's no diamond mine, it's a very large drug laboratory, MDMA and Ice apparently.'

'Are you on a sat phone', came the immediate question.

'Yes, Sir', Pete responded, 'I'm being careful what I say. I have others with me, including Andrew who is injured and two foreign nationals. Not sure yet how we are going to get out of here.'

'I may be able to help there', offered the Admiral, 'we have your old friend Succeed a ways off to your West and I'll point her in your direction. We have been trying to get diplomatic clearance for a routine port visit but their officials are stalling for some reason. If things get too hot press the SOS button on your phone and that will give us an excuse, but wait at least 24-hours so we can be reasonably close. Meanwhile, the requirements are evidence, destruction and safe return.'

Both had finished their respective phone conversations and Alison had started tipping over various containers to the obvious panic of the distraught Luis.

'We must get out', he yelled 'that stuff's dangerous', and made a bee-line for the doorway. He was recaptured with ease by Pete, who also realized the guy had a point. There were now chemicals and miscellaneous liquids starting to cover the floor of the building, so he guided Andy and his lady-friend outside with Luis and called for Alison to retreat.

'We need to be thorough', argued Alison heatedly.

'Diesel!' That thought came to mind as he remembered the diesel generator next door.

'Can you hold him?' This directed to Andy who was clearly not in good shape. His return nod was good enough, and Pete raced next door to grab what diesel fuel he could. That took the form of a half-empty drum which he had no difficulty rolling into the main building and tipping its contents on to the rest of the gelatinous mess on the floor.

'Ok, smart-ass, now how do we get that alight?' queried Alison pointedly, 'you going back in there to commit suicide?'

'You're not the only one with gadgets', responded Pete smugly, and fished into his back-pack for the flare gun. He confidently loaded and aimed at the diesel with the gun going off with a whoosh. Nothing else happened except a red glow in the room.

'Aim for the cardboard packaging', suggested Alison.

The repeat performance was a minor initial success with the packaging catching alight and slowly spreading. There was soon a good degree of flame but little else until the diesel caught. That quickly produced a major fire, with the walls of the building soon alight and the building's complete destruction almost assured.

'They're going to see that in the village and the Chief's team will come running', declared Andy with a worried frown.

'If that's the cruiser's crew they left last night', announced Alison, 'we will need to get to the barge.'

'But that will have left by now as well.' This was Tamika's first contribution since Pete's arrival and he looked more closely at her. A very attractive young woman, he thought, and for the first time guessed that she and Andy were in some kind of relationship.

'The barge is going nowhere', said Alison proudly as she waved a bunch of something in the air, 'I have the keys.'

'And if they have a spare set?' enquired Pete cynically.

'Well, I pulled the ignition fuse too. They will take quite a while to find and fix that', she added smugly.

With flames roaring behind them and smoke billowing, the four bedraggled but hopeful escapees and their prisoner headed down the track toward the village. Luis was giving no trouble and seemed completely cowed. They had gone about two kilometres, footsore and, except for Luis, thoroughly weary, when out from a group of trees came the Chief. He pointed a pistol confidently toward them and yelled at them with evident anger.

'Stop right there', he began, 'you, drop that rifle', pointing the pistol at Pete. 'You people have no idea what you've done. Do-gooders unable to leave things alone and spoiling the future for everyone. Anyway, you will all pay, so keep heading down to the village and don't try anything stupid as I would happily shoot the lot of you right now. Maybe I'll make an exception for you Luis, but you had better have a good story or its curtains for you too.'

Pete placed the rifle on the ground and moved backward to protect Alison, except that she had disappeared. He moved over to the others and they all moved forward cautiously and with depressed looks. Suddenly there was a movement at the left-hand side of the track as something either fell, moved or was thrown. The Chief instinctively turned in that direction as Alison burst from the right-hand side behind him and grabbed him around the arms. The Chief pulled the pistol's trigger but it sent up a spurt of coral only a metre or so in front of him. As he let out a frustrated roar, Pete leapt toward him and took over his seizure. The Chief fought and struggled but Pete was a relatively strong man, albeit with little patience at that moment. He punched the Chief hard in the kidneys and that ended the struggle. More of Alison's cable ties neutralized any further aggression on his part.

Approaching the village an increasing number of villagers silently lined the track, though not making any move toward them. That was until they were close to the centre of the village adjacent to the marked police hut. There a larger group stood across the track barring their forward movement. The Chief took his opportunity.

'These people have destroyed the mine and put all of your futures into jeopardy', he yelled. 'None of you will be able to get an education in Australia', he added gesturing to a group of the older students in the assembly, 'they are terrorists! They have no concern for the damage to the islands their people are causing and they care nothing for you. Stop them!'

Tamika took the initiative and stepped forward. 'He lies', she spoke confidently and loudly so that all could hear. 'There is no mine and never was. These two', she pointed at the Chief and Luis, 'have been manufacturing drugs and selling them overseas. They are criminals. Ask yourselves why every move you all make is controlled by the Chief and his thugs. Ask yourselves why there are young children on this island who are not allowed to see their parents. Ask yourselves why we don't get any tourists here anymore. You all know in your hearts there has been something wrong here for a long time. Now is the time to fix things. We will ask the police to investigate properly and bring this island back to being its old happy and carefree place.'

There were murmurings all around, but plenty of nods of agreement and no overt disagreement. Pete decided not to await any second thoughts to develop and pushed their two captives forward. The islanders parted and let them pass, which made Pete pause slightly as he didn't know the way to the barge. Alison solved that difficulty by leading the way and they were soon in sight of the disabled barge.

'What was that about children being held here?' Pete looked at

Tamika as he asked, but it was Andy who responded.

'There is a group of about five or so younger children here who don't get to see their parents', he said. 'They each have parents in high places in Rarotonga. I can only assume that they are being held here as some sort of protection against police or government interference in these drug operations.'

'We must take them home.' Tamika could be very forceful for one so young.

'Assuming they want to go', Alison wisely added. 'Where do we find them?'

'I will go bring them', said Tamika, and she headed off to the school where they would just be assembling.

'Our next issue is the barge crew', reported Alison, 'they are not going to be a happy bunch.'

That was less of an issue than anticipated. The skipper and his crew were sitting disconsolately on the wharf. The skipper glowered at Alison and spat 'You're late, but lucky for you we can't go yet. Engine problem, engineer fixing now.'

'My friend here is an engineer', she lied whilst nudging Pete in the ribs and slipping the keys and fuse into his hand. 'Maybe he could help?'

There was a grunt from the skipper, who gestured lazily for Pete to help himself aboard. Fifteen minutes went by until Pete reappeared on the barge bridge looking like he had been working in a coal mine.

'Fixed', he yelled, 'ready to start up.'

The skipper looked disbelieving but went aboard and a few minutes later the engines roared into life. Meanwhile, a disoriented group of schoolchildren had appeared on the wharf, looking up at the barge expectantly.

'They all come', declared Tamika proudly.

'What's this then', the surly skipper yelled from the wheelhouse wing as he watched the schoolchildren and small group of adults clamber aboard, two at least obviously unwillingly.

'They are coming with us', declared Pete as he ostentatiously pulled the Chief's pistol from his trouser band. 'You can cast off straight away and take us all to Manihiki at best speed.'

'Like hell they are', argued the skipper who was about to say more when Pete lost his cool and delivered a massive uppercut to the skipper's chin. Fortunately, Alison had his hands bound behind him with her apparently endless supply of cable ties before he could respond. She looked up at Pete.

'Can you drive this thing?' she questioned.

'I can drive anything that floats', boasted Pete and he took over the wheel and throttles as they manoeuvered away from the wharf.

Just then the HF radio at the back of the wheelhouse crackled and they heard 'Pacific barge this is Blue Turtle, over.' After a short silence the call was repeated, then 'Pacific Barge, this is Blue Turtle, come in you dull loser or you'll regret it.' Pete decided to answer and grabbed a cloth from the chart table 'this is Pacific Barge', he covered the mike and replied with a rough and muffled voice.

'Have you left the island yet?' was the retort.

'No', Pete answered.

'Good, the Chief is not answering his calls, get someone up there, no, better still you go up there and let him know we got his message. We have turned back and should be there in a bit over an hour.'

'OK', was all Pete felt he needed to say and rushed over to the barge skipper. 'How fast can this thing go?'

The barge skipper was still truculent and in no mood to cooperate but still quite proud of his vessel. 'Seven knots, maybe a touch more if she's pushed.'

Pete pushed the throttles all the way forward and did some rapid calculations over at the chart table. 'Shit!' he exclaimed.

Alison and Andy came over together and asked in unison 'what's the problem?'

'They are going to catch us. We need the police; I think it's 999 here.' he added and promptly dialled. As he did so he noticed the SOS button, and recalling his conversation with the Admiral, pressed that too. After going through the usual preamble, he asked to speak urgently to the captain of the police patrol boat and after another minute he came on the line.

'How can I help Captain?'

'I am on the Pacific barge between Rakahanga and Manihiki', Pete explained, 'we have your Police Chief's son onboard together with a group of other senior officials' children. We are being chased by armed thugs in the local cruiser Blue Turtle.' Pete was placed on hold for a few moments whilst Jacob seemed to be talking to someone else.

'Captain, we are a bit south of the Northern Group at the moment and now altering for Manihiki but it will take us the best part of three hours to get there. This better be for real, Captain; we will stay in touch on Channel 17, that's still public but probably less used than others.'

'Thanks Jacob, I'll give our position hourly.'

'Tell me exactly what the issue is please Peter?' Alison realized that this was more Pete's domain and was happy to defer to him.

'We are about 26 miles from Manihiki', Pete began explaining, 'that's 22.5 nautical miles and at seven knots that will take us around three hours. My guess is that cruiser could easily be doing sixteen knots so they have a nine-knot advantage over us. Assuming they turn for Manihiki as soon as they realize we are not at Rakahanga, then they will catch us before we can make port. That could be disastrous.'

# CHAPTER 20

During the course of Peter Martyn's telephone conversation, the nearest Iridium satellite had detected the emergency signal from his phone, including its GPS position, and relayed that information to a series of ground SAR stations throughout the South Pacific. In turn that information was broadcast to maritime units within a reasonable distance of that location. These units included the Australian warship 'Succeed' which turned to approach at high speed.

'Succeed' had been having a fairly easy time of late, a short 'flag showing' visit to Fiji the previous week and a loitering role to the West of the Cook Islands awaiting diplomatic clearance for a visit to Rarotonga. Daily internal drills were taking on a routine of their own and there was a relaxed atmosphere throughout the ship. Commander David Bell had settled into his new command role with ease and presently sat comfortably in his bridge chair with a bacon sandwich in hand. That had been a victory of sorts, getting Steward Goldman to produce his favourite breakfast.

'Sir, you have a call on the sat link from maritime headquarters', this on the intercom from the communications centre. 'Can you come down please Sir, it's a bit awkward to patch it through.'

'On my way.'

He clambered down the ladderways to the communications centre to be offered a seat in front of the Satellite terminal. 'Commander, this is Admiral Usher. I need you to extract Captain Martyn from whatever trouble he has got himself into. I briefed him to activate an Iridium SOS if he was in dire straits, so that's what the situation must be. The chances of another Iridium SOS from that region around now are almost zero. So, your orders, Commander, are go get him. Liaise with their Guardian Class patrol boat if you can, they might be responding too.'

That was all quite straightforward thought David, although what he might be responding to was as clear as mud. Back on the bridge he called the navigator over and checked the charts, whilst telling the Watch Officer to increase to 30 knots.

'We are in a pretty good position skipper', advised the navigator, 'the GPS position is just off a Rakahanga Island which is about one hundred miles North of us. Should take a touch over three hours.'

Discussions followed with the Executive Officer to have a boarding party briefed in case of need and an instruction to the operations room to see what they could do about contacting the Cook Islands police. There didn't seem much more he could do until he knew what they were facing, David thought. Then a call came through from the operations room.

'Getting traffic on VHF skipper, a vessel calling itself Pacific Barge just reported its position to what we think was a police patrol boat. The position given was about seven miles South-East of Rakahanga.

'Adjust course please Watch Officer', David ordered. He then called his Executive Officer back to the bridge to discuss their legal situation. They were well inside Cook Islands Exclusive Economic Zone and as yet had no clearance for a visit to the country. The saving grace was an SOS call which warranted a response from any vessel capable of doing so, but they would have to be careful about what they did when they got there. The pair of officers agreed on a cautious approach to any action. Then Ops called again.

'We have established VHF with that Pacific Barge skipper; they want a phone number.'

David gestured to Steward Goldman who had just appeared with a cup of coffee for him and asked him to go get his cellphone from the cabin. This done, and number passed, he was soon in contact with his surprised ex-captain.

'I gather you are in a pickle of some sort Peter', he ventured, 'what gives?'

Pete explained his situation briefly and David then suggested he turn the barge due South to increase the closing rate. That done, it became a wait and watch game as the distance separating them progressively diminished. Nearly two hours passed before any further development.

'Surface contact on radar, twelve miles due North', reported Ops, course 180 speed seven.'

Ten minutes later the tension levels on the bridge were rising steeply.

'Two new contacts', reported Ops, 'one smaller contact about one mile behind what we are calling the barge and another larger contact fifteen miles South-East. Course on the latter North-West at about twenty knots.'

'Let's be prepared like proper boy scouts', David said to no-one in particular, 'man the Vickers.'

The 'Vickers' were twin machine guns mounted on each side of the bridge.

'Shots fired', came through the VHF, 'they are using rifles, no hits yet.'

The three converging vessels were now getting close, the barge now being less than a mile ahead.

'Come down to twenty knots', called David, 'I have the con.' By this he meant that he would personally control the ship's movements directly rather than the Watch Officer. 'Clear all upper decks.'

He steered as close as he could safely do toward the barge and then, as she was passed, brought the ship into a tight starboard turn, then reversing course almost as soon as he passed the barge's stern. The warship heeled dramatically and stirred up an enormous series of waves in her wake as she settled behind the barge.

'I want a burst of fire in front of that cruiser', he called, 'make sure you don't hit her.'

The frigate was now between the two ships and a burst of fire from the starboard Vickers brought up spurts of water in front of the cruiser. The smaller vessel weaved violently and came to a near halt, rolling alarmingly.

'Ten knots', called David as the frigate weaved across the gap between cruiser and barge.

The VHF burst into life again, this time on the bridge Channel 16. 'Warship to my south, this is the Cook Islands vessel Blue Turtle, you are interfering in the capture of a stolen vessel and abduction of Cook Island citizens, stand clear.'

David worried that they may have entered into a possible political bun-fight over this, but was instantly relieved as the VHF came back to life. 'Blue Turtle, this is Cook Islands Police vessel. Stop your vessel immediately and prepare to be boarded. Pacific Barge, you stop also. No vessel is to engage in any provocative action.'

That didn't quite produce the desired reaction. Blue Turtle suddenly surged ahead trying to get around Succeed and peppered the barge with rifle fire. A second burst of machine-gun fire from the warship gave the cruiser crew reason to reconsider and she then turned sharply, increased speed and headed off to the North. A calm descended on the remaining vessels as they remained stationary awaiting the police vessel.

Thirty minutes later the main participants were gathered on the deck of the barge and getting or giving briefs. Jacob listened carefully to what Pete explained of proceedings to date and was visibly relieved when he recognized both the Prime Minister's and Police Chief's offspring among the children gathered on deck. 'Well, this mess is going to take some sorting out and I will, of course, require formal statements from each of you. Meanwhile, I guess we all have some calls to make', he acknowledged. 'I will put two of my officers on the barge to Manihiki and we will take charge of these sorry-looking individuals', he added nodding towards the two captives and the barge captain. 'I have a well-trained crew to handle the likes of that Blue Turtle crowd so I will be heading straight to Rakahanga where I fully expect to find both her and her potentially interesting cargo.' He then turned to David and asked formally if he would escort the barge to Manihiki. 'There will probably be quite a few VIPs from Rarotonga there by the time you get there to discreetly thank you guys', he noted, 'but don't expect any detailed publicity. They won't want to acknowledge any perceived flaws in our "Diamond of the Pacific", however temporary!'

# CHAPTER 21

To suggest that Andrew Martyn's life had since become more complicated would be akin to asserting that Einstein's relativity theories were straightforward. The complexities had increased, as they are often wont to do, when he sat down with a lawyer.

'Let me make sure I understand this Mr Martyn', began the solicitor with the unexpected Cook Islander name of Albert, 'you arrived in the islands over two months ago; you have no money and no identification and you would like to stay and work here, although you have no job.'

'That about sums it up', responded Andy succinctly. 'Let me explain. I was kidnapped by a group operating out of Rakahanga Island who are now before the courts. I am an Australian Navy Commander based in Port Moresby but my intention is to resign form that position to stay here. During my initially unwilling stay in Rakahanga I came to like the place and incidentally happened to fall in love with a local lady. We now wish to live together, for which I need work of some kind.'

'If you had not been introduced by Jacob, I would think this a most improbable story and a doomed objective', commented Albert. Jacob, the Coxswain of the Rarotonga police vessel which had arrested the key players in the drug supply ring, had kindly given him a lift to Rarotonga to sort out his situation and introduced him to Albert. Jacob had left him with a caution to keep much of the detail to himself as the government would not appreciate any significant publicity over the affair.

'In the simplest of terms', Albert continued, 'you are technically an illegal immigrant and liable to immediate deportation.

Were that to occur, you would then be subject to a three-year exclusion order. Now it happens that persons with diplomatic credentials are exempt from deportation so, if you can confirm your status, we will obtain some breathing space. As for remaining here permanently, let alone working, that presents difficulties. You would need to identify a reputable employer and establish that you possess specific skills otherwise unavailable. From my experience with such matters Mr Martyn, approvals are rare: you would probably need the personal intervention of the Minister to be successful.'

Andy had left the solicitor's office with his head spinning. He had taken a room in a small hotel whose management had demonstrated remarkable Cook Islands hospitality by taking him in on the promise of full payment 'as soon as practical'. A reverse-charge phone call to Angela, his PA in Port Moresby, whom he then discovered was working for his brother, had her welcoming him back to the world. He had apparently just been formally declared missing, although his brother had already phoned in with a brief summary of their adventures. Temporary identification documents would take a few days, so his next stop was Central Police Station. The police were none too happy about his plans to depart in the near future as he was required as a key witness in the forthcoming trial of the alleged drug ring. Happily, it transpired that the Chief of Police discovered that he was in the building and came to congratulate him on rescuing his son who had been held hostage on Rakahanga. Learning that Andy was required to return to Port Moresby but intended to ultimately seek residence in the islands he smiled broadly and waved away the police prosecutor's objections. 'We can't stop him leaving anyway', he had noted, 'Commander Martyn holds diplomatic status.' The one item of particular good news for Andy was that a search of the Rakahanga group leader's accommodation had discovered Andy's passport and wallet, although minus any cash or credit cards.

Feeling like he was facing the music a few days later, Andy found himself again in a police headquarters, though this time in Port Moresby. The detectives listened carefully to his story of abduction and the surrounding activities of the drug supply organization, including his being alerted to an arms shipment aboard the motor cruiser 'Blue Turtle'. His explanations apparently tallied with other evidence that they had accumulated so he was removed from their list of suspects regarding an associated homicide.

There remained more loose ends to tie off; not the least being the Navy and his wife. The former was relatively simple: he wrote a letter of resignation which Angela faxed to Canberra for him, although he was required to stay 'in office' at the High Commission for a further month until a relief could be arranged. His brother Peter had since left for Sydney after filling all involved in on his own and Andy's exploits although, for some reason no-one quite understood, he had travelled via Hong Kong with Alison Ho. In any event Pete had clearly given a glowing report on Andy's performance so he was being regarded around the Commission as something of a battered hero. His wife Christine was going to be a more challenging proposition.

Andy was unsurprised to learn that Christine had been charged and was currently remanded in custody for alleged drug supply. Their relationship had been rather frosty for some years. More recently he had also been suspicious of her mood changes and the occasional arrival of mysterious parcels. He felt a degree of self-recrimination for not having resolved those issues before now. Disappointingly, he also realized that only Christine and Angela knew that he had departed for Rabaul to pursue the 'Blue Turtle' so one or the other had arranged, or at least triggered, his abduction. He was quite certain which woman it had been. Now, he had to face her.

'Hello Christine', he began confidently as he approached the lady in question in the prison visitors' area. She still looked the gorgeous woman he had long been attracted to, despite the tousled hair and dull grey jump-suit she was wearing.

'I hope you're not here to gloat', she had responded, 'so just don't start. You have no bloody idea what it's like to be left alone all day in a foreign country with no friends and nothing to do. So, don't come the high and mighty with me you bastard.'

'I'm glad to see you too Chris', Andy retorted sarcastically. 'I simply came to see how you are coping and perhaps address our future.'

'We have no future Andrew Martyn, at least not together. If I survive this hell-hole I never wish to see you again, except perhaps in a divorce court.'

That had been the end of that conversation and Andy returned to the office to investigate and sort out what might be left of his personal belongings. They had apparently been packed, boxed and placed in storage at the High Commission. He didn't have much. Accordingly, it didn't take long to identify the few items he would really like to keep and set the rest aside for the tip. The exceptions were a black briefcase he didn't recognize and a large envelope of what seemed like property deeds. He took the briefcase back to the office and unsuccessfully fiddled with the locks. Eventually he decided brute force was the only realistic option and searched around for a suitable instrument. A large screwdriver fitted the bill and he stared into a briefcase neatly divided into many bagged compartments. Opening one he poured out what looked like a greyish mix of different sized rocks. Diamonds? He didn't know what raw diamonds really looked like so he stashed the briefcase under his desk and took one bag together with the property deeds down to the resident AFP officer, his friend Phil Stroud.

Phil was an experienced police officer and took only a brief glance at the 'rocks' before declaring them to be raw diamonds. 'You have quite a little stash here, Andy, worth a few thousand I'd say, where did they come from?'

'Stored with my things in the store-room; not sure I've seen them before myself. Maybe they were Christine's, although she didn't say anything about them to me.'

'Well, they are yours now I suppose', replied Phil, 'unless of course you want to have them declared as lost property. I wouldn't hold out any hope of them doing anything except disappearing in that case though. What else have you got there?'

Andy passed him the envelope of deeds and Phil took a great deal more interest. 'These are all property titles for houses in Cooktown', he noted, 'the titles are all vested in "The Hahalis Society of the Cook Islands" whatever that is. These are only copies of the title registration of course, but you could still sell a house based on one of these. They are quite valuable documents; you should keep them somewhere safe. I wouldn't mind taking a copy though, if you don't mind, the Cook Islands have been cropping up in official correspondence quite frequently lately and these may have some relevance.'

Some weeks later, the High Commissioner spoke well of him at a short farewell tea, any of Andy's previously alleged misdemeanours obviously forgotten or forgiven. The Navy had provided a final air ticket "on retirement" to Sydney, which he had promptly converted for a flight to Rarotonga. Now with access to both his backpay and superannuation benefits Andy was in high spirits. These were elevated further by a phone call to his lady-love Tamika who apparently awaited him with delight on Rakahanga.

Andy's first port of call on arrival Rarotonga was his previously doubting and pessimistic solicitor Albert. To say that there was a marked change in his attitude was an understatement.

'Welcome back Mr Martyn, so pleased to see you again', Albert began as he ushered him warmly into his office. 'You clearly have friends in high places Mr Martyn; may I call you Andrew?'

That agreed, Albert continued 'well Andrew, there is a little-known element in our Immigration Act which makes provision for what is termed "Honorary Permanent Residents". This is for persons who have made a notable contribution or done a great service to the Cook Islands. It would seem that not only the Chief of Police but none less than the Immigration Minister himself believe that you qualify for that honour. The formalities are in process as we speak. Congratulations Andrew!'

'That's great news, thanks. Any idea when I might know the outcome?'

'I'm sure they will have a decision before your current limit of thirty days is up', Albert pronounced assuredly.

'There is one other matter, please Albert. What do you know of the "Hahalis Society of Cook Islands"?'

'Never heard of it, but it should just take a minute or two to find out', he responded and bent over his computer. It took barely a minute before he leant back with satisfaction. 'Found it', he said, 'it's a registered charity. Aim given as being to further the wellbeing of Cook Islanders by charitable works.'

'So, who would the trustees be then', queried Andy.

'It just gives the trustees as "those appointed from time to time by the members", read Albert.

'Obvious next question Albert, who are the members?'

'Reasonable question, but the answer is a bit vague. It does state that "members shall comprise all Cook Islanders over the age of twenty-one years whose place of residence is registered as being on the island of Rakahanga". No names are listed.

'Fascinating stuff, Albert. I'll be on Rakahanga until required back here, thank you.'

Andy had a two-hour gap before his scheduled flight to Mani-hiki to catch the barge to Rakahanga and so diverted to the wharf area. Having met up with Jacob, the skipper, he was invited for coffee and when suitably settled he enquired about when Jacob thought he might be called to give evidence. 'I'm not sure you will be required at all', advised Jacob, 'the prosecutor has cut a deal provided they all plead guilty. It seems he is under pressure from on high to keep a lid on the whole saga. That's going to make life a lot easier for all of us and some of the main players will get deported in the end anyway.'

'You'll let me know whichever way it goes?' queried Andy and received a confirming nod in response. 'As a matter of interest, what's happening to the "Blue Turtle"?' Andy added.

'Ah, sore point,' Jacob pulled a wry face. 'Actually, it's an embarrassment. It's been seized as the proceeds of crime. The Government want rid of it but there no buyers for that sort of vessel around here. You interested?'

'Could be, provided I get permanent residency', Andy replied, 'how would I go about buying it?'

'Not sure at this stage, I'll mention your possible interest, but if there aren't any offers, I suspect it will probably end up in the Police lost property auction in a few weeks' time.'

With that, the pair bad farewell and Andy headed for the airport.

His arrival at Rakahanga was celebratory to say the least. His lady-love jumped onboard before the barge was properly secured and hugged him fiercely. It seemed that most of the village was gathered around the wharf area and there were cheers and whistles to applaud Tamika's actions. Tamika led him ashore possessively and up to a well-dressed woman standing slightly apart and looking every inch the lady.

'Andrew, I would like you to meet Mrs Patricia Green; Mrs Green is the local Member of Parliament and Leader of the Opposition. She has been away from the island for some time now for personal reasons.'

'I am delighted to meet you Mrs Green', Andy began, not sure what to make of this unexpected development.

'The pleasure is mine', the lady responded, 'I and my family have been living under threat for a very long time now, and I am informed that it was your actions here that ultimately removed that threat. I owe you a debt of gratitude Mr Martyn. If you need help in any way, I would be only too pleased to assist.'

The rest of the way to Tamika's hut was taken at a leisurely pace and Tamika made a more personal welcome once inside. The rest of the evening and beyond were spent in a loving and very physical fashion. Life was becoming a touch less complicated and the future potentially quite rosy. He glanced idly around the hut when his wandering eyes stalled on a framed embroidery with the letters TS. Tamika, he thought. 'I've just realized, my love, that I don't know your second name', he murmured.

'Sopolo', she answered simply. 'I thought you knew'.

'You mean like the "Chief" Sopolo'? he questioned.

'Yes, of course, Michael is my father'.

Andy went rigid with shock. He was in bed with, and by all his own reasoning in love with, the daughter of an imprisoned drug lord who had been about to have them both killed.

# CHAPTER 22

Time was rolling on and Captain Peter Martyn was becoming a trifle bored. In his role as staff officer at Naval headquarters in Sydney he planned a lot, he coordinated a lot, but he didn't DO a lot. He was becoming prone to self-reflection. He was still reasonably fit and managed a few kilometres of jogging each week; well, indeed very enjoyably, married; and with three healthy, happy children. Having lost his first wife to a murderous attack a few years previously he had met his new wife in dramatic circumstances in the Cook Islands, although she was actually of Chinese heritage. They had enjoyed a whirlwind romance in difficult circumstances as they recognized that one or the other needed to abandon their homeland and associated culture for them to remain together. As it transpired, this was prospectively less dramatic for his then-fiancée to relocate than it would be for himself. He still felt an unease, though, about having uplifted her from her familiar surroundings and career. The happy arrival of a son of their own to add to his existing offspring of twin girls had definitely eased any tensions that may have arisen. If there was something missing from his life, he couldn't quite put a finger on it.

Alison Martyn, ex-Detective Inspector of Hong Kong Police, was also becoming a trifle bored. She had fallen quickly and deeply into a quagmire of love and lust for this tall, good-looking and serious-minded but very caring Australian. Equally she realized that she had probably reached the zenith of her police career and, whilst deeply respecting her Chinese heritage, was more aligned with the old colonial values of Hong Kong than the more recently evident mainland mind-set. Alison remained very fit and active, often to the wonder and admiration of her new husband. The children occupied much of her time, happily so. She filled in some gaps with teaching evening classes in Tai Kwon Do, in which art she easily maintained her high black-belt grading, and running occasional half-marathons on weekends. If there was something missing from her life, she couldn't quite put a finger on it.

That evening over a quiet weekend dinner, with children tucked away in bed, Alison was fiddling with a large tube of skin balm. She looked up at Pete and innocently enquired 'would you like more children Peter?'

'I'm quite content my darling girl, how about you? Do want another joyful bundle of nappies and sleepless nights'?

'I too am content Peter, maybe even thinking of going back on the pill. How would you feel about that?'

'I think I am as happy as I could ever be', he answered, 'we have three gorgeous children and we have each other. Why want more, and why worry about the future?'

Alison was idly scanning the ingredients of the balm she held. 'We must always think of the future Pete, we have another three little lives to think of. And you know what? We could make this stuff! Look what it's made of', and she threw the tube to him across the table.

He caught and examined the incoming missile with surprise, disinterest and not a little disdain. 'Lavender, Calendula, Bergamot and Beeswax', he read aloud, so what?'

'I believe we need to stretch ourselves a bit Peter. I have things to do here at home and you have your work but we don't do much together these days. That is not to say I'm unhappy, because I'm not but are we going to stay content in our little domestic bubble? I would love to see us take on a challenge together and this balm stuff might just be the ticket. My forensic experience and your organizational skills might just make it work and we could have some fun along the way.' Alison finished and looked at Pete expectantly.

She now had his full attention and he perused the contents of the tube of balm more closely. "I know virtually nothing about women's cosmetics', Pete commented, 'nor men's cosmetics for that matter. It would certainly be a challenge if that's what you're after. We could buy in some of the ingredients but we would probably need to produce some of our own to make it viable financially. Maybe we would even need a small property. I would have to think about all this a bit more. Could you give me a week or so?'

Two weeks later and the matter was close to being settled. Pete arrived home with a broad grin on his face to be met with a laughing Alison at the door, also apparently eager to share her news. 'You first', he said.

'I think I've found a place!' She didn't so much say that but let it excitedly burst out of her.

'Well done you', he acknowledged. 'For my part I have been checking options and I'm told if I take accumulated leave plus long service, I end up with over four months leave available. That should be plenty to decide whether we are going to make a fist of something new. First a drink please, then you can tell me about this discovery of yours.'

'Near a place called Milton,' she exclaimed, 'it's nearly twenty acres mixed pasture and woodland and it's got over a thousand olive trees on it already. The house isn't much, just two bedrooms made of what they call weatherboard but we could fix that up. There are sheds and everything', she finished happily. Actually, she hadn't finished. 'It's up on the computer and available for viewing over this weekend', she ended, almost pushing him over to her desk.

'Ye gods and little fishes Alison', you see the price on this place?' Pete was startled by the outrageous figure posted on the advertisement. 'I'm not sure we can afford that on my salary.'

Undaunted, Alison stared at him and declared 'sometimes Peter I really think you believe you married some poor stray Chinese waif begging for crusts on the street. I have more than enough money stashed away than either of us are ever likely to need.'

'You are not talking about that bag of ill-gotten rocks you've hidden in the closet are you?' Pete was referring to a bag of unpolished diamonds she had "confiscated" from a drug dealer's house in the Cook Islands during the escapade in which they had met.

'Not at all', she fired at him, 'that's awaiting a good cause for the Islanders one day.'

That settled, and having arranged to meet the Estate Agent, they prepared to head off that Saturday.

Pete froze when he saw her ready to depart. 'By all the Gods Al, you can't go visiting a country town looking like that. You'll cause a riot!' She was wearing a fashionably short skirt, loose blouse with no evident bra and killer heels. With her sleek black locks neatly hanging down her back, long and equally sleek legs, high cheekbones and well-considered make-up she looked like a high-end fashion model about to embark on the cat-walk.

'Ah dad!' This in unison from the twins staring adoringly at their beautiful new mother.

'Could I perhaps suggest some slacks and lower heels?' Pete ventured. 'You do look quite gorgeous though, Al, and I would be proud to walk around any city on earth with you like that.'

Costume adjusted, they cruised down the coastal highway to meet up with the estate agent, who turned out to be a very pleasant middle-aged woman. It took relatively little time for them all to be chatting and smiling at each other. A firm sale was in the offing, although Pete made a point of questioning the price and was given to understand that the vendor was retiring and quite flexible. They agreed to let her know a decision in twenty-four hours and headed into Milton proper. Pete paused outside an ice-cream shop.

'Do you think we can we still afford a treat for the girls?' Alison smiled benignly and he headed inside. Heading back out no more than a few minutes later with a handful of ice-creams he was met with quite a sight. Alison was kneeling on a very large disreputable-looking man with her hands at his throat. She was surrounded by a small crowd of onlookers clapping and cheering. Alison rose sheepishly as he approached and got in first. 'He grabbed my arm, called me a "chink" and asked if I wanted a "quickie" she explained, 'he's obviously drunk.'

An elderly and well-dressed man wearing a tweed jacket and hat came up to Alison, touched his hat and declared 'that was magnificently done young lady. You just had the misfortune to meet up with our local nuisance drunk. I'm the local Mayor and you've just done the town a good service.' Thank you', he added as they all eyed the malcontent wandering in shock down the pavement. No-one noticed the young lady on the opposite side of the street with her ubiquitous iPhone filming the episode.

The trip home was filled with the twins excited chatter about their heroine mother's amazing put-down of the "nasty man" as they termed him. Alison simply raised her eyebrows and smiled at Pete's questioning looks.

The girls were now old enough to be included in family discussions and took on serious expressions as they pondered whether they wished to live in the country. Those expressions lasted but fleetingly as they burst into a gleeful chorus of 'can we?' Decision made! A deposit was placed electronically the next day and both Alison and Pete celebrated with a large brandy. The girls' protestations were ignored as they were instead offered lemonade.

Pete looked around at their existing but still very new house. It had been built on the rubble of his previous home which had been destroyed, together with his previous wife, in a deliberate explosion set by foes of his brother. It held only sad memories except for those accumulated with Alison. 'What do think my love, do we keep this place or sell it?'

Alison snuggled up to him on the sofa. 'Why would we want to keep it?' she asked. 'We won't need this place and the extra money might come in useful for our new venture.'

Having yet another decision made, action was swift. Real estate agents appraised the house, offering values way above Pete's expectations, and the house was on the market within a week. Within a further fortnight, the house was sold.

Excitement mounted exponentially within the Martyn household as the time for their move approached. Then the bushfires swept through together with mysterious phone calls.

# CHAPTER 23

If Christine Martyn thought that she was lonely and friendless in the diplomatic circle of Port Moresby, that state could be considered happy fulfilment when compared to the situation she now found herself in. The confines of Bomana Prison on the outskirts of Port Moresby were, to any intelligent woman used to a comfortable lifestyle, absolutely soul destroying. To one who had never bothered to familiarize herself with local language, customs and ways of socializing, the inherent misery of imprisonment could be, and actually was, exacerbated many times over. A considerate guard had provided her with a grey jump-suit for her visit from her husband, but she had now been forced to revert to the worn skirt and blouse she had been arrested in.

She looked around the outdoor exercise yard at the miscellany of other prisoners, all lazing in the heat of the day and all indigenous Papua-New Guineans. Except, she now noted, not all were! Similarly dressed in an opposite corner of the enclosure was another white woman. She seemed to be confidently chatting to a couple of locals. That she needed to make that woman's acquaintance was self-evident to her. It took another day to achieve that but then she managed to catch the woman alone.

'Hi, I'm Chris. Nice to meet a fellow Euro', she began, but got no further.

'Waddya want Martyn?' The woman sounded as rough as she looked and clearly not a conversationalist.

'I would just like to talk to someone', she said, 'and you clearly know who I am'.

'I know everyone here of any significance, you're just one of many.'

Chris decided to get straight to the point. 'I need to get out of here. Any ideas?'

'What's in it for me?' was the immediate response.

'Come along with me.' Chris wasn't very hopeful of a really positive outcome but that's exactly what she received.

'I can get out of here all by myself', the woman said, 'but can you get me out of the country as well?'

Chris thought for a few moments. 'Yes, I'm fairly sure that I can, I would need a few days advance notice though.'

'I'm Marge', said the woman in an entirely different tone, 'follow me'. With that the pair strolled across to the far side of the enclosure and sat down, leaning back on the wall. There was an immediately watchful guard eyeing their movements but as they were making no further suspicious moves he was soon distracted by more interesting sights.

'Here's how it's going to work', announced Marge, 'you ever used Betel Nut?' After Chris had shaken her head, she continued 'good, one of us is going to have a heart attack. They take patients straight to the town hospital and normally put a female guard with women, but they are usually pretty relaxed when away from the prison and it should be easy to get away from her. I think it's best if I do that bit, because the one who gets out has to come back here and I don't trust you enough to do that. For the next few days whenever we are outside, we both come over and sit at this exact spot. The guards will become quite used to that happening. You will have to scale that wall in front of the wire. The same night I get out I will come back here and cut the wire upwards about a metre. You come back to this spot the next day, maybe two. I will need to organize a car and some clothes so it might be the day after, but I'll whistle if all is in place and off we go.'

'Sounds simple enough, but I'll need to make a phone call', said Chris somewhat dubiously, 'how do I do that without giving the game away?'

'Got any money?' asked Marge quickly. 'I'll need at least a few hundred dollars.'

Having agreed arrangements, the pair sauntered back to afternoon "lock-up" under the watchful eyes of the armed sentries. The next morning a guard came to see Chris and informed her to head to the main office for her phone call.

'Anders, this is Christine. Ivor is in Port Moresby and wants to meet you here for dinner this Saturday evening', she lied. 'You could bring your mate Austal and his little brother. Can you make that?'

Anders was the gang's Cooktown distributor and if there was one person on this earth who could make Anders decidedly nervous it was the group's 'hard man' Ivor Slavinski. He was not to know that Ivor was uncomfortably housed in Rarotonga prison so would probably go out of his way to comply.

'Christ, he doesn't make things easy', he answered, 'when and where?'

'It has to be this Saturday, say 8.30pm. There is a great spot about ten kilometres south east of Moresby called Canoe Coffee. Ivor suggested a beach romp afterwards.' Chris was hoping Anders would have the sense to realize that she was being deliberately vague but with sufficient information for him to understand. Austal was the brand of Anders' offshore fishing vessel and by mentioning his little brother in the context of a beach he should appreciate that she meant a pick-up by dinghy. If the prison staff were monitoring her call, they may just disregard it as having little real significance. If they were aware that Canoe Coffee didn't open for dinner on Saturday night she was in trouble.

'OK, I'll be there', Anders grumpily agreed, 'but he had better understand that this is a one-off.'

That Wednesday night was a sleepless one for Chris, whose nerves were strung as taut as a violin's and she wondered whether she was really able to pull this off. Late the following morning she met up with Marg and they strolled to their usual spot. Marg sat and started discreetly stuffing her mouth with chopped Betel nuts. Nothing happened and Chris began to think nothing would, when Marg said 'now!' and fell to the ground clutching her chest. Christ stood and screamed as loudly as she could. She obtained the satisfaction of instant attention from all around.

'Help, help, please. My friend seems to be having a heart attack'. Sure enough the signs were pointing that way. Marg was sweating and having visible tremors, then began vomiting, all the while groaning and evidently in pain. It took a few minutes for the guards to organize themselves and another five or six minutes for an ambulance to arrive, but Marg was eventually carried away and their plan was in motion.

The next twenty-four hours were terrifying. Chris had always been the backroom woman for the drugs group and had never been involved in any of their more overt physical activities. Sitting all afternoon in their designated spot was simply awful, just waiting and waiting. Nothing happened and she started to think she had been set up. The next day was Friday and maybe their last opportunity. After another sleepless night the day began the same way as before. Standing and stretching occasionally to keep her muscles from tightening up completely she began to think how gullible she had been. Then a soft whistle from behind the wall. Could that have been a bird? No, it came again, a little louder this time. Chris was on her feet in an instant and walked slowly away from the wall. She then turned and ran as fast as she could to leap at the wall and scrabbled at the bricks to get leverage. Her arms were burning and she was close to complete panic as she just managed to get her torso over to the top. She fell in a jumble of arms and legs next to the outer fence. A rifle-shot sounded from one of the guard towers and she was showered with pieces of brick and mortar. Pulling herself together she sighted Marg gesturing frantically a bit further down the fence and she scrambled towards her still feeling panic-stricken. Through the fence and she was grabbed by Marg who started almost dragging her toward the greenery a little further away.

'We have to get across the river; quick, we'll need to go like the clappers', Marg yelled as alarm sirens began to sound from behind them.

'A river?' Chris questioned in breathless alarm.

'The Laloki', yelled an equally breathless Marg. 'They won't expect that cause of the crocs, but there is a shallow patch that we can be across before anything gets stirred up'.

Chris half ran and was half dragged. There was hardly a pause as they entered the river. Chris's heart was racing and her mind numb with fear as she entered the surprisingly cold water. A gasp of sheer terror escaped her as she dropped into a deeper patch and the water came almost to her shoulders. Scrambling up the far bank she was uncertain whether she was relieved or still in the midst of a nightmare. The journey continued through an orchard and a grove of trees for a few hundred metres, with her being, and definitely feeling, wet and bedraggled. They came quite suddenly into the open and a dirt track where a battered and tired-looking Volvo sat idling quietly. Its local driver was sitting, patiently waiting without expression.

'In the back and get your head down', yelled Marg as they jumped in the car, which roared off without delay. It slowed to a more sedate pace as they progressed through twists and turns that made Chris nauseous, although she wasn't able to identify whether the cause was the car's movements or delayed shock. Either way, they eventually approached a small village and pulled into what at first appeared to be a derelict house. If any of the locals watching thought it unusual for two white women to be in this part of town and with one looking like a scarecrow, they made no comment.

'We stay here the night', stated Marg, 'there's some clothes in the back room that should fit. You will find a shower on the back verandah.'

Cleaned up, Chris was feeling mildly better, probably just relief she thought. She mentioned again that she needed to get to her old house. 'Risky, I know, she added, 'but necessary if we are to get clear.'

'Tonight, after dark' was all that Marg offered, and they both settled down, hoping the inevitable outcry over their escape would pass them by.

The afternoon and evening passed peacefully, with some staple foods to keep them occupied, although Chris had the appetite of a sparrow. An hour or so after darkness fell, they heard the Volvo draw up outside. Marg looked hard at Chris and explained 'you don't need me with you for this, but don't try anything silly. The driver is an old "wontok" of mine from the highlands and he'll happily slit your throat if he senses anything not right.'

Chris had no idea what a 'wontok' was but got the message. The driver took the journey to her old residence carefully and without conversation. Arriving, she looked around the vicinity very slowly to assure herself that they were alone. Satisfied, she went around the back and checked for occupants: thankfully none. Forcing the back door, she climbed on to a chair under the loft access. There she retrieved an old shopping bag that looked ordinary enough but contained her private escape kit. She rifled through the contents: a thick bundle of Aussie dollars; passport, driver and birth certificates, pre-paid mobile, a torch and her loved but unused Glock 43 9mm pistol with a full six-round magazine. Hurriedly putting the manhole cover and chair back into place, she searched unsuccessfully for her briefcase and returned to the car feeling annoyed but much more in control. The trip back to their temporary residence went smoothly and her confidence grew a little more.

Marg said nothing when she arrived back but her body language spoke of relief. They sat through the rest of the evening and next morning in near silence and Marg would not allow a radio. She really didn't want Chris knowing that her prison guard had been knifed, probably fatally, during her hospital escape. 'It should start getting dark around 7pm so that's when our driver should be back. You'll need to pay him upfront tonight', she added, 'I promised him a thousand Kina, that's a bit over $400. Can you afford that?' she finished with a questioning look.

'Sure, no problem, although it will be in Aussie dollars', Chris responded, and they both settled back into silence.

Before the sun went down Chris changed into a pair of slacks and a dark well-worn jumper she found in the back room. Her nerves were jangling yet again as 7pm approached. When it did, with the sun dropping to the horizon like a stone, the Volvo reappeared and they set off. They had gone no more than a hundred metres when the driver stopped and held out his hand. Chris counted out $450 and passed the notes across. Nothing was said and the car moved off. By 8pm they were at the café carpark and searching for a way down to the beach as their car disappeared into the night. It proved to be a struggle, but eventually they were down and staring into the marine darkness. They had one of those waits where each minute seemed like an hour. Then a quiet yelp as Marg saw it first and pointed. The navigation lights of a small vessel approaching the shore were now evident and Chris flashed her torch in that direction. She repeated the process in a series of flashes every few minutes until they were both alerted by the noise of an outboard. A dinghy was soon seen nudging itself carefully toward the beach, then grounding.

A large man came up the beach shouting 'Ivor?' in a questioning tone. 'Here!' responded Chris and moved forwards.

'You're a woman', the man shouted, then even more querulously, 'my God, two women! What's going on I'm supposed to meet a man called Ivor?'

'He sent me and my friend instead', replied Chris forcefully, 'let's get going'.

'I can't do that', I'll have to go back and check with the boss', was the stern response.

Chris quietly pulled the pistol from her shopping bag and, whilst pointing it directly at the man in front of her, shone the torchlight on to it to make her point clear. Unsurprisingly he acceded to their request to board the dinghy and they were onboard facing Anders within minutes.

'No questions Anders, I'm not sure if you know exactly who I am but I run Ivor's business. I'll explain everything when we get to Cooktown and also make sure you're not out-of-pocket for this little trip. So, off to Cooktown Anders, and don't spare the horses.

Amid much head-shaking, Anders returned to the wheelhouse and navigated out to sea. Meanwhile Chris found a comfortable spot on the back deck and, before settling down for an uncomfortable journey, was promptly seasick. That remained the status quo for the next twelve hours until berthing discreetly at Cooktown wharf.

# CHAPTER 24

It was a pleasant sunny morning with the thermometer nudging 25C and forecast to rise another six or seven degrees. The balmy wind was a currently pleasant North-Westerly but increasing in strength quickly across New South Wales. A disregarded log that had been quietly smouldering after a lightning strike a few days earlier suddenly burst into flaming life. It was the start of a bushfire that began seeking food for its flames and had a voracious appetite. This fire was not fussy about the fuel it consumed and had no regard for human values; it consumed all in its path; trees, shrubs, houses and even people. If it met something flammable it would burn. Its pathway of destruction was as predictable as the prevailing wind and, in this case, it was headed directly for the property that Peter and Alison Martyn had set their own sights on. The reality was that there were fires all along the east coast of Australia, it was that time of year after all, but this was the only one that warranted their individual attention.

Peter was at work, having been called in to coordinate Navy's response to the East Coast fires with helicopters and firefighting logistics. He heard the name Milton cropping up occasionally on the broadcasts, but took no special notice: he was busy. Alison was also busy, but in a more domestic sense calming her fractious one-year-old son and was paying more attention to the radio. She called his mobile.

'Pete, there is a fire heading for our property near Milton', she reported. 'Is there anything we should do?'

'Sorry Al, not much we can do about it', he responded, 'and it's not actually our property yet. All we can do is hope the present owner is ok and has the place insured'.

As it transpired, the owner was ok and very relieved to have moved his possessions out the previous week. It must have been a close call for he was still very shaken when he spoke on the phone. Pete let him know that they would be down to see the damage and talk things through that weekend.

Approaching Milton along the highway they could see little evidence of any bushfire damage. Then they turned on to the back roads and a horrified silence descended on the car. Even the twins became very quiet. An enormous swathe of blackened trees, burnt grass and the occasional pile of bricks and corrugated iron that used to be someone's home covered the landscape. Alison, whose entire upbringing had been in the urban environs of Hong Kong, was having difficulty understanding the scale of destruction and becoming quite emotional. There were tears gently rolling down her cheeks, and even Pete was choking up as he thought about the losses involved. Entering their prospective driveway, they came to a rapid halt and simply stared – there was virtually nothing there.

The house had clearly borne the brunt of the fire and was completely destroyed. The owner, standing morosely next to his battered utility, was little better.

'Thirty years I've lived here', he said shaking his head sadly, 'all but the last with my late wife. God I'm glad she never got to see this. The house is gone as you can see and most of the paddocks, but the olives only got scorched around the edges so they'll be ok', he finished. He then looked up 'what do you want to do about the sale?'

Pete took charge and led the distraught man over to their car where they had a flask of coffee.

'Were you insured?' was the immediate and rather direct question from Pete.

'Oh, yes' was the simple reply.

Pete was well aware of the legalities involved but also sympathetic. 'Why don't we wait until you know what the insurance company will pay; you keep that and we will pay you the rest of the agreed price,' suggested Pete.

'That sounds very fair', noted the owner looking somewhat re-lieved, 'that may not cover any clean-up costs though.'

'How about we cover those from what we are likely to save in State Stamp Duty', added Pete.

With that they parted and the Martyns took a final drive around the main paddocks to survey the damage whilst also realizing that they would have some fencing work to do as well. Still, Pete thought, that would not do his fitness levels any harm and they would eventually get the place as they wanted it. Meanwhile, they surveyed the devastation. Doubtless the flames would have been seen by any witness as having arrived through an opening in Hell. What they left behind was Hell's de-tritus: a dull kaleidoscope of black and grey ash as far as the eye could see.

'Well my love, are you still in agreement to go ahead?'

'I'm quite content Pete', Alison said quietly but frowning, 'we were going to rebuild the house anyway, so I'm feeling a touch guilty about that, but now we have a problem. Our own sale still needs to go ahead as we are contracted. That means we will have nowhere to live in a few weeks' time.'

The drive home was uneventful and they turned into their own street ready for some rest and quiet reflection. The bevy of parked cars and milling cameras outside their house augured otherwise.

'What on earth is going on here?' queried Pete, with a few ex-pletives thrown in. 'You guys best stay in the car until I find out what's happened', Pete added as he parked in the driveway.

What had happened was a function of modern social media. The girl who had filmed their encounter outside the Milton ice-cream shop had enjoyed checking her phone record of what she saw as a successful expression of the women's fight for respect. She eventually uploaded an extract to YouTube. A few others had enjoyed the vision and shared it with friends. The video had gone "viral". The small press gathering was clearly wanting an interview with the heroine of the piece and that placed Pete in

151

a quandary about how to respond. He first explained to Alison what seemed to have occurred.

'There are two ways we can play this Al', he said, 'we can tell them all to piss off, in which case they will hound you for a week or two. Alternatively, you can take their questions in a more comfortable spot. How about I ask them to give us a few minutes to get settled and then the come inside, perhaps the back verandah, and ask away? How would you feel about that?'

'Ok', replied a bemused Alison, 'as long as they leave the children out of it.'

Comfortably seated on the back verandah, Alison posed for a few photographs and answered politely a disparate series of questions ranging for women's rights to racial harassment and self-defence training. With their appetite for a newsworthy story satisfied, the press departed, Pete poured them each a Gin and tonic and they settled down to a peaceful evening. That lasted until the evening news.

For reasons known only to a collective of news editors, the story of Alison's 'put-down' of her assailant in Milton was carried by almost every news channel. It was true, though, that her well-spoken and cultivated Oxford speech combined with her good looks and intelligent responses made for good copy. That was inevitably followed by opinion pieces in the next morning's newspapers. Then the phone calls began. Some were complimentary, some critical and a few, very few, distressing. Then came two from entirely unexpected sources.

'Pete, we've been invited to tea at the Chinese Consulate', announced Alison excitedly. Pete was less thrilled. 'What, me too?' he questioned. 'We'll need a baby-sitter.'

'An au pair or Nanny would be better!' Alison retorted from the kitchen.

A second call was less social and a bit disturbing. 'Pete, it's Christine'', Alison announced as she handed him the phone.

'Hello Chris, I thought you were stuck in Port Moresby', he started diplomatically.

'I am still in Moresby', she lied, 'but trying to sort my personal belongings out and there are a few things missing. I'm missing a black briefcase and a folder of personal papers', she asserted, 'have you got them or know where they might be?'

'Sorry Chris, I didn't go back to the house at all after we parted, so I've no idea. Surely someone in the High Commission would know.' Pete was in minor turmoil: he was still emotionally affected simply by hearing her voice but his conscience was doing cart-leaps.

'They are being their usual unhelpful selves', she opined, 'but thanks, I have to go now. Bye.'

# CHAPTER 25

Christine ditched Marg almost immediately after landing in Cooktown and headed to the 'Vinnies' store in town where she purchased a change of clothes. She paid cash for a ticket to Cairns and arrived in that city the same day. Ensconced in a neat motel, it hadn't been difficult to get the number of Peter in Sydney and she had been mildly disappointed when a woman had answered. Well, if Pete didn't have her briefcase, and she believed what he had said, then that left Andy, whom she had already suspected. Now to begin her move toward vengeance for all the hurt that man had caused her over the years and with a new life of personal freedom.

It was still the tail-end of holiday season and there were plenty of tourists and an associated night-life in the city. She was accosted by optimistic men half a dozen times that evening before she eyed her first prospect. The bar was dimly lit and noisy, with couples gyrating on a central dance-floor. The woman was blonde, not too far removed from her own age and standing alone at the bar. Chris went straight to the bar, stood next to the woman and waved for the barman's attention.

'Whiskey please', she ordered, 'best make it a double.' She turned to the woman beside her who was nursing a stale beer and offered 'want to join me?'

'Sure, this was horrible, a whiskey too please', the woman responded.

Drinks having been served, the two women began the idle chatter by which people begin to know each other.

'Do you live here or just visiting?' queried Chris.

'Oh, just visiting for a while. Broke up with my boyfriend down in Sydney, more fool me', the woman informed her. 'My parents didn't approve and since they still hold the purse strings, I went along with their wishes to keep the peace. They shouted this holiday for me as compensation'.

At the mention of close parents, Chris cooled the conversation and made her excuses after they had finished their drinks. Two more similar bars were investigated before a new option presented herself. She was probably a touch younger than Chris but of similar build and appearance. She was seated at a table away from the dance floor by herself. Chris stood in the shadows for a few minutes watching her movements, or rather lack of. Satisfied that the woman was alone, she made to pass by that table and apparently slipped as she did so. Searching for support she grabbed the edge of the table, which promptly tipped, spilling the woman's drink on to the floor.

'I'm so terribly sorry', Chris claimed with as much sincerity as she could muster, 'can I get you another drink? Please let me compensate', she pleaded with a smile.

'Ok, that would be nice, thank you.' That began a long conversation over multiple drinks and the woman explained her solitude.

'I was working in a bar down the road until the owner decided I should reward him in bed', was the aggrieved explanation. 'So now I'm out of work and in a town with no friends and few prospects at this time of year.'

Chris placed her hand over the woman's in apparent sympathy and held it there. The woman's hand was not withdrawn.

'Want to dance?' Chris asked and received a shy nod in response.

The dance-floor was dimly lit and the music had now lowered in volume and tone to a slow and sadly romantic blues-style of tempo. The two women held each other lightly and swung gently to and fro with the rhythm. After a little while and as they were each clearly taking comfort from the embrace of the other, Chris gently kissed the woman's neck. She received a murmured 'nice!' in response.

'Want to go somewhere quiet?' was an unanswered question as the woman took Chris's hand and led her outside. They ended up after a short taxi ride in a small second-floor apartment near the waterfront. Chris and the woman, whose name turned out to be Anne Turner – 'Anne with an E' – as she had put it humorously, made love to each other at first gently, then more frantically. They ultimately collapsed in panting exhaustion and lay curled up together in mutual satisfaction and comfort. The night wore on as it is wont to do and the two women enjoyed ever more adventurous love-making until dawn made its presence known through the curtains.

'My shout for breakfast', declared Chris brightly as she headed for the shower, with a sleepy response happening somewhere behind her.

Showered and dressed, they both enjoyed a large and filling breakfast in a local café, during which Chris discovered all that she needed to know about Anne Turner.

'I have some things to do back at my place', Chris declared as the table was being cleared, 'but how about we go for a drive this afternoon and just talk?'

That sorted, Chris went back to the motel and sat down to write a thoroughly sad note on motel notepaper which she carefully folded into an envelope. Using some of the motel's cheap hair shampoo she rubbed her eyes until they were sore and went below. She paid the bill looking sad and teary and arranged for a hire car to be delivered to the motel. Paperwork duly completed in her own name and using her own credit card, albeit now invalid, she headed to the nearest shops for a local map and some more appropriate clothes. Now dressed in a bright yellow, very short, skirt; flat country-style shoes and blouse with no bra, she headed off to meet Anne.

Once in Anne's apartment, the girls kissed spontaneously. 'How are you feeling about last night?' questioned Chris, looking directly into the woman's eyes with a warm and slightly lascivious smile on her face. Anne's response was to lean forward, kiss her gently and place her hands under Chris's blouse whilst fondling her breasts. Within moments they were on the lounge-room carpet having frantic sex, still only partly unclothed. Breathless but opportunistic, Chris asked if she might stay with Anne, perhaps for a few weeks. Anne agreed happily and Chris arranged to pay the rent once she found out to whom it was paid.

Driving South on the highway, both women were in carefree mood. Chris turned off on to the coast road, looking for a service station where trucks stopped. Once she had sighted a likely looking place, she veered off on to a side track into national park and stopped next to a steep ravine, ostensibly to admire the rather limited view.

'Let's walk a bit', she suggested and Anne got out of the car with her. Chris promptly retrieved her shopping bag of goodies and discreetly withdrew the pistol, just in case. Drawing Anne to her she kissed her gently on the forehead and said softly 'turn around'. With Anne still in front of her she began caressing the back of her neck to occasional sighs from her victim. She now reached down and picked up what looked like a stout branch, stepped back and swung it with all her strength into the side of Anne's head. Anne dropped to the ground apparently life-less. Chris quickly knelt and checked for a pulse and was satis-fied with the negative result. Turning the body over, she made doubly sure by smashing the branch into the front of Anne's face, ensuring both death and a complete facial disfigurement. A quick search of Anne's clothes revealed little. She removed her own wedding ring and placed it on Anne's ring finger but baulked at losing her fine diamond engagement ring. Lifting the body carefully so as not to get any blood and gore on her clothes, she launched the body as far as she was able down the ravine.

Back in the car, Chris drove forwards until the car was pre-cariously placed facing into the ravine and carefully removed all trace of Anne together with her handbag. Placing her own small handbag, which held her driving licence and a mixed bag of personal papers, on the front passenger seat, she added the envelope simply addressed 'farewell'. That done she went to the

rear of the car and pushed with all her might. It looked initially like the car would stubbornly resist its destruction, but
eventually it moved forward, gathered momentum, and hurled
down into the ravine. Now for the hard part, thought Chris,
and she scrambled down into the ravine, carefully avoiding the
tyre tracks. Her bare legs were quite scratched by the time
she reached the car and she was thankful for the forethought
in wearing sensible shoes. Opening the driver's door wide, she
leant in, started the engine and put the car into forward gear.
The vehicle was firmly held up against a towering gum tree and
moved forward not an inch. Chris left it like that and struggled
back up to the track, then paused both to regain her breath and
check for unwelcome visitors.

Chris, who forcefully reminded herself that she was now Anne,
had a five hundred metre walk to the service centre she had
identified. Entering, she surveyed the scene and noted what
looked like a truck-driver in shorts and thongs tucking into
chips and coffee. She composed herself, ordered a coffee and
took a seat at a table directly opposite the truckie. Making sure
her bare legs and short skirt were obvious, she glanced up as he
got up to leave and asked 'you going into Cairns by any chance?'

The truckie looked her up and down before answering. 'You
really shouldn't be hitch-hiking looking like that', he admon-
ished, 'but if you want a lift, you're welcome.' The pair left together and Anne introduced herself, telling the driver that her
fiancé had angrily ditched her out of town and with no other
means of getting home. On the relatively short drive there were
plenty of sideways glances at her undoubtably attractive and
rather sexy appearance but nothing else. To her surprise she was
dropped off in the main street with no further comment or invi-
tation. So much for the reputation of truckies, she thought.

Back in the apartment the new Anne contemplated a thorough
search through the previous occupant's belongings to solidify
her own identity but thought better of it. A stiff drink to settle
her nerves and a good sleep would suffice until the next day.

That next day and six more passed before the body was found.

Natural decomposition, aided by rain and animal activity, had made simple identification impossible. The detective called to the scene examined the body, read the note and decided that suicide was sufficiently clear not to warrant detailed investigation. He prepared a report for the coroner accordingly. When police files elicited the information that the victim was an escaped prisoner on an international wanted list, the detective informed the AFP in Canberra with professional satisfaction at another loose end being tied up. The one outstanding element was informing the next of kin and when the husband was ultimately identified and found to be both separated and overseas, that confirmed his personal verdict and the case was closed.

# CHAPTER 26

Mornings sometimes bring a clarity of thought with their cooler temperatures and hint of fresh beginnings. There was little sign of that happening this particular morning: Andy was in a distinctly confused state of mind. A brisk walk up the village track did little to help mentally, but did remind him of his deteriorating level of physical fitness. Sighing, he sat down, leaned against the trunk of a coconut tree beside the track, not a usually recommended practice, and began some deeply introspective thinking.

His thoughts drifted back to his early career and how it began. He had joined the Navy partly out of some enthusiastic encouragement from his uncle and more so from a desire to follow the footsteps of his elder brother Peter whom he idolized. Peter was the gung-ho, seagoing adventurous type, but Andy had soon realized that a life at sea was not really for him and he had focused increasingly on shore-side activities. In this current moment of self-reflection, he also realized that he was impulsive by nature but also prone to drifting through life. He had let events steer his course rather than directing that course to meet his own ambitions. The classic case had been his marriage to that witch Christine, he thought, which had caused immeasurable heartache ever since, not least due to the cold antagonism he met from his brother.

Andy's marriage to Christine had been based upon a lie. She had arrived at his flat one night in tears announcing her pregnancy. It became clear that the child couldn't be Peter's as he had been away at sea for over three months. Equally, he knew with absolute certainty that it wasn't his, but whose was doubtful: Christine was perhaps the most promiscuous woman he had ever known.

"I will tell everyone it's yours", she had declared miserably, "you will look after me, won't you?'

Why Andy had ever agreed to that was one of his life's unanswerable questions. Certainly they had slept together in the past, but not since she had become engaged to his brother. She had all the hallmarks of a successful young woman who would make anyone an attractive and personable partner. He had also thought to protect his brother from what would, he was sure, be a marital disaster that could possibly destroy the man. Had he slept-walked his way into a miserable marriage of convenience he asked himself. Probably was his own conclusion. It had been two years into the marriage before he had discovered that Chris was actually infertile. Damaged fallopian tubes caused by a teenage case of chlamydia apparently. Clearly there had been no pregnancy in the first place. They had stuck together, though, tied by bonds of sex, disillusion and the occasional bout of mutual depression. That Chris had resorted to drugs he had little doubt.

Was he about to repeat his failures, this time with Tamika, he wondered, or was this a continuum of him drifting along as the tide took him? In a moment of determined positivity, he decided to find out.

'Tamika, we need to talk about us', he stated forcefully as he stalked into their hut. 'What is it that you want from me?'

Tamika looked perplexed. 'Why should I want anything from you that I don't already have?'

Andy launched, rather disconsolately, into a statement of where he thought they were at. 'I am a married man, nearly a decade older than you; I have no job and when my visa expires in ten days I may be expelled from the islands. My wife is in prison, so I am unlikely to be able to get a divorce any time soon, and your father hates me enough to want to kill me. Is there anything I've missed?'

Tamika looked closely into his eyes and saw a tormented soul.

'Do you want me Andrew?'

'I want you more than you could know', he responded, 'but I could ask you the same question'.

'I want you Andy. For now, I have you. For me that is enough', she declared in her usual staccato fashion.

'But how about marriage, children, a life together? When I first arrived you said you would like to get pregnant and go to Australia. What happened to that? The real question for me is do you love me enough to give everything else up?'

'I wondered when that word "love" would arise', she said quietly. 'You westerners use that word a lot. You love food, you love your parents, you love going to the beach, you love almost anything that pleases you. For Islanders love is very serious, it is enduring and it involves an attraction beyond the physical.' For Tamika that was almost a long speech and she was not finished. 'Andy I may love you, but I would never admit such powerful feelings unless I become certain that the feelings are mutual'.

Andy was momentarily struck dumb. He needed to be sure that what he said next was not another case of foolish spontaneity. He became sure. 'Tamika, I love you', he said simply and held his breath.

A broadly beaming Tamika gave the game away before she spoke. 'In that case the feelings are mutual Andy, I love you too. Maybe now we can sit down and work out the rest of it.'

They sat together over a celebratory lunch of pulled pork and rice discussing their options.

Tamika managed to surprise Andy a little more. 'Maybe we should write down a Harvard Decision Tree?'

He looked at her in mild wonder. 'So how do you know about those?' he asked.

'I'm just a simple Island girl who happens to have a bachelor's degree in business management', she announced. 'My father insisted upon it very early on and I finished it on-line by the time I was twenty-four', she added proudly.

'Wow!' Andy could find no other words that properly expressed his surprise and pleasure.

On that note they nutted out a rough plan of action based sensibly on taking one step at a time. A first step was resolved more quickly than expected. Walking to breakfast together the next morning they met Patricia Green coming towards them.

'Well my brand-new constituent has saved me a short walk', she began, 'is there somewhere we can talk?'

'We are off to breakfast', Andy announced, 'why not join us?'

'Happy to', was Patricia's pleased response and they headed down the track together.

Once seated and having had at least a few sips of coffee each, Patricia looked across the table and announced 'I have good news. Earlier this morning I received a message from Avarua. The Cabinet has determined that a certain Mr Andrew Martyn, having provided important service to the Cook Islands has provisionally been declared an honorary permanent resident of the Cook Islands'. She waved down Andy's attempted joyous leap from his chair and continued 'now you need to know that this is a very unusual situation. I can only make guesses as to what that service was, but it is clear that no publicity will occur. I am required to advise you that you are expected to personally honour the confidentiality of the relevant circumstances behind the declaration or it could be rescinded. If I have your agreement to that then I have to message back and the arrangement will be finalized.'

'You have my agreement', declared Andy without hesitation.

'Patricia stood, leaned across to Andy and shook hands. 'Congratulations', she said, 'I'll get on with the formal response and you should get the paperwork shortly. I mean "shortly" in Cook Islands' time', she added with a chuckle.

'One thing before you go Patricia, if I may call you that?' enquired Andy tentatively, 'what do you know about the Hahalis Society of the Cook Islands?'

'Firstly', Patricia began, 'you may not call me Patricia: Pat will be fine, thank you. As to that other name, I've not heard it before.'

'Oh, I know about that', chipped in Tamika 'I helped set it up. It was one of my father's bright ideas; a charity established mainly for poor people on Rakahanga. I put the deeds together for him, but I doubt it ever went any further, there were no assets nor income and so no charitable works possible, at least as far as I know.'

Later, Andy and Tamika went for a swim off the beach then dried off in the warm sun. They lay together sleepily then Andy rolled on his side and asked 'have you still got the deeds to that charity, Tamika, or know where they might be?'

'Father's office I suppose', Tamika responded disinterestedly, 'it hasn't been touched since he left. The police searched the place I think and took away some guns and things, but all his paperwork should still be there.'

'You might be surprised to learn, my lovely and loving business partner, that the Hahalis Society seems to have property registered in its name in Australia.'

Tamika was dismissive. 'Name coincidence', was all she said and promptly rolled on to her stomach and ignored him. 'Oh, alright', she exclaimed petulantly a few minutes later, 'if you're determined to spoil my beach time, let's go and search the office.'

Searching the office revealed little, but before leaving Andy pointed to an old iron safe in the corner.

'Oh, I don't have the key to that', asserted Tamika, 'we will have to wait until my father gets back'.

That set Andy back on his haunches. 'What do you mean when your father gets back? He should be in prison for a long time and why would he come back here anyway?'

'He was only charged with weapons offences', pouted Tamika, 'pleading guilty he was only given twelve months of prison and with good behaviour he'll be out in a few weeks' time. Why wouldn't he then come back here? This is where he lives.'

Andy was stunned. He was starting to realize that perhaps he had not thought through his situation as fully as perhaps he should have.

# CHAPTER 27

Pete walked into his Admiral's office expecting to give a routine brief on what were now post-bushfire recovery operations. What he got was a seat in a comfortable chair, a cup of coffee and a boss who was appraising him carefully.

'I have been looking over your Cook Islands report again', the Admiral began, 'you seem to have struck up a bit of a friendship with their patrol boat skipper'. Pete's intended response was waved away and the Admiral continued, 'and an even closer friendship with the lady who is now your wife. I need to ask, Peter, how well you really know Alison Ho and her background? Before you answer that I must inform you that your security clearance is presently under review. You have married a Chinese national, made an unannounced visit to Hong Kong and are now known to have visited the Chinese Consulate here in Sydney. You must know that for an officer in your position all associations with foreign nationals need to be fully reported. So, don't be surprised when I tell you that certain people in Canberra are taking an interest.'

Pete could almost consciously feel his blood pressure rising. 'The lady's name is Alison Martyn, not Ho', he almost spat, 'and I know her well enough to be certain that she poses no issue warranting Navy's or our security service's attention. I would have thought the same consideration would apply to me.'

'Relax, Peter', the Admiral said soothingly, 'I'm just telling you like it is, but let's get back to the patrol boat skipper. How well did you get to know him?'

This conversation took a few more unexpected twists and turns before the Admiral stood and said 'Peter, I want you to know that I'm on your side. It does seem, though, that things have been taken out of my hands. You have been reassigned for special duties, whatever that means and are to report to a Charles Donnelly in Canberra on Monday. Here are the details', he added as he passed across a slip of paper. 'Meanwhile, why don't you call it a day and go home?'

"Home" was now a rented a four-bedroom weatherboard on the outskirts of Sydney. Pete unlocked the front door to be met by Emily, their newly acquired nanny, and two overactive girls fresh from school.

'Daddy, Alison's going to teach us Chinese', announced the girls in unison.

'By "Alison", do you girls mean "Mummy"? questioned the more conservative side of Pete.

'No daddy, Mummy died: now we love Alison', responded the confident Samantha to assenting nods from sister Rebecca.

Well, that sorted that, thought a bemused Pete as he turned to the nanny. 'All well Emily?' he queried lightly, 'where's Alison?'

'Probably on the phone', Emily responded, 'I certainly wouldn't like to pay your phone bill'.

'Really?' Pete was doubtful. 'Who on earth has she been ringing?'

'No idea', was Emily's nonchalant response, 'it's all been in Chinese anyway so I wouldn't have a clue. Same with the visitors, they spoke Chinese too'

Pete wandered into the bedroom to find that, sure enough, Alison was on the phone. A peck on the cheek and a raising of eyebrows elicited no response other than a distracted 'be with you soon darling'.

In the post-dinner peace of the evening, Pete gently eased himself into the subject concerning him. 'So, what do you think about these goings on in Hong Kong?' he asked.

Alison was thoughtful for a moment then reminded him that as a police officer as she then was, her views were not necessarily objective. 'But', she added, 'Beijing's intentions are pretty clear, so it is wise for residents there to think carefully about whether they are determined to be democrats or can live as Communists. There is an old saying', she added, 'when the wealthy leave somewhere, it is time to pack: when the poor leave somewhere it is too late. I left and I am happy about it.'

'So, what are all these phone calls in Chinese about?' Pete queried.

Alison chuckled. 'Emily has been telling tales, has she?' A very Australian trait, Pete thought: answer a question with a question! 'I've been drumming up business for the Dojo', she finally answered dismissively, 'and I've also been talking to some other Chinese people about teaching English, but I'll apparently need to get a local qualification to do that if I want to get paid. We don't need the money but I would enjoy the distraction.'

'Well, I have a distraction of my own for you', Pete offered, 'I have been re-assigned and my security clearance is being reviewed. Don't know much about it yet, except I have to be in Canberra next Monday. I suspect it's to do with our marriage but I would expect that you might get a bit of a grilling from our security people at some stage.'

Alison sensed an opportunity. 'I've already had that, your ASIO people I think they said, but they seemed to go away satisfied. Anyway, I need to visit Canberra myself at some stage, so maybe I could come with you.'

Pete, somewhat reluctantly, agreed and they drove to Canberra on Monday morning. Alison asked to be dropped off at the Chinese Embassy, which set off even more alarm bells, and he proceeded to his meeting with the mysterious Mr Donnelly in what turned out to be at the Attorney-General's office building.

Pete was confronted by three senior public servant types in a fairly large office: two youngish men of medium build and pale office-bound complexion with a middle-aged woman dressed casually and with somewhat unkempt hair. After brief introductions which said almost nothing substantive about what those people actually did, he was unexpectedly but thoroughly questioned on his Cook Islands' experience. The topic then took an even more surprising turn.

'What to the terms "Fox Hunt" and "United Front" mean to you Captain?' queried Charles Donnelly. Receiving a completely blank look, he continued 'how about "Belt and Road"?'

Pete explained the little he knew of China's ambitious raft of infrastructure projects, apparently aimed at reinvigorating East-West trade routes along the lines of the ancient "Silk Road". On completion of what was a relatively short discourse, Charles looked at his fellow, albeit silent, interrogators who simply nodded. A buff file was slid across the table and Charles continued 'That is some briefing material for you. We are keen to know where the Chinese investments in the Cook Islands are heading and in particular any proposed port developments. We want you to go there and have a nose around. You will keep your Naval salary and we will cover reasonable expenses. Who "We" comprised wasn't explained but billing was apparently to be addressed to a section of the Attorney-General's Department.

'Oh, one last thing Captain', added Charles, 'we want you to take your wife. You could make it a family holiday perhaps.'

Pete left the building feeling confused. He rang Alison to arrange to pick her up for lunch and the journey home.

'I'm outside a large building called the Ben Chifley Building', advised Alison.

That building, Pete knew, housed ASIO, the security and intelligence organization. Unsurprisingly their lunch together and the journey home kept Pete particularly quiet and thoughtful. When he broached the subject of a holiday back to the Cook Islands, Alison seemed unsurprised and entirely positive. Her concerns, if any, seemed to revolve around what to do with the girls. The added role of looking after the twins full time in their parents' absence didn't seem to phase Emily, but her quoted fee was astronomical. A little bartering and the prospect of a tropical holiday resulted in decreased fees and increased smiles all round. Within the week the whole family and nanny were on their way to Rarotonga.

# CHAPTER 28

Anne Turner, aka Christine Martyn deceased, was fretting at the ponderous progress of bureaucracy. With artfully applied make-up, her "lost" driving licence was replaced without difficulty but a new passport was taking much longer. She had been unable to find one in her predecessor's belongings, if indeed she had ever held one, so she had to begin the process from scratch. Eventually, some three weeks later, the shiny new blue passport arrived in the mail and Anne was ready to move. Her cash reserves were dwindling fast but, having been Ivor's confidante and occasional lover, she well knew where she could find some. She headed by car to Cooktown, enjoying the relaxed freedom of her new identity.

The property she was navigating to was easier to find than she expected from the description previously given her by Ivor. The gated entrance and overhead sign "Hahalis 2" confirmed her expectations and she pressed the attached intercom.

'This is Christine, Ivor Slavinski sent me', she reported into the intercom and the gates slowly drew open with no verbal response. At the front doorway she was met by a large Islander woman of middle age.

'You must be Moana', Christine suggested, and received a nod but a not-so-warm welcome. 'I have been asked to get a progress report and examine the Register', she stated with more confidence than she felt. Moana seemed to be cooperating but Chris felt the need to confirm her credentials. 'You have an assistant, do you not, is that still Janice?' she asked.

'Yes, but Janice is not here at the moment', Moana lied, 'she is checking on the young ladies nearing term'.

In the spacious office, Moana slid a leather-bound Register across her desk and looked up expectantly.

Flipping open the Register to the last filled-in page, Chris glanced at the final balance and demanded: 'and the cash? I need to check it.'

Moana knelt in front of a large old-fashioned safe, opened it and stood back, clearly inviting Chris to examine the contents. This she did but was forced to kneel to peer into the darkened interior. She saw neat bundles of notes and was about to reach in when she felt sharp steel pricking her neck.

'Don't move a muscle', Moana threatened, 'I happen to know that Christine Martyn is dead. It was in the local papers. So, who are you really?' she demanded. 'Show me some ID!'

Chris slowly rose to her feet, thinking fast but with the knife or whatever it was still firmly pressed into her neck. 'In my handbag', she spluttered, pointing to the bag now resting on the desk. She reached carefully for the bag and opened it. Thinking that perhaps this larger woman was not as agile as herself she then dropped straight for the floor, rolled and pulled out her pistol. Undaunted by the weapon now facing her Moana lunged forward with the knife. She was met with a resounding "crack" and instant chest pain as the pistol fired but she managed at least a wound to her assailant's shoulder as she collapsed.

'You bitch', yelled Chris as she kicked Moana in the ribs and reached to staunch the blood now oozing from her shoulder. The door was suddenly flung open and the supposedly absent Janice stood frozen at the sight greeting her.

'Move over to the desk', demanded Chris as she aimed directly between Janice's eyes. Chris was in early shock and with her pulse and mind racing equally. Maybe this was an opportunity. 'Turn around and face the wall', she added to Janice. Reaching for Moana's knife, a wicked-looking stiletto possibly used as a letter opener, she thrust the knife into Janice's kidney area. Spinning her around she struck again, this time aiming for the heart and was instantly gratified as the light left Janice's eyes. Re-arrangements were now called for. The two bodies were placed facing each other on the floor, with Chris reluctantly giving up her pistol to place it firmly in Janice's hand. Wiping the handle on a tissue, the same thing then happened with the knife, this time in Moana's hand. Satisfied that she had set the scene as close as was possible to resemble a dual killing, Chris emptied the safe of potentially useful paperwork and cash, grabbed the Register and hightailed it to her car.

A helpful chemist provided the necessaries to dress her wound and ease the pain, whilst a travel agent in the same complex joyfully arranged her "holiday" to the Cook Islands. Chris made a firm resolution to embrace her new identity and she was on her way to Rarotonga.

This place is as hot and humid as Port Moresby, she thought as she entered the Rarotonga airport and caught a taxi to the resort her travel agent had booked. A soak in a warm soapy bath and a body massage relaxed her and settled her into "island time". She reviewed her options, all of which required a substantial amount of money. The $12,000 she had recovered from the Cooktown facility was mere seed money, she thought. Another island nation, maybe: perhaps Fiji or Tuvalu sounded like good retirement options, even Vanuatu. But first a good night's sleep and then to business.

A taxi took her to the reception area of Rarotonga Prison, where she asked to visit Ivor Slavinski. Frisked and denied her phone, she met him in the visitor's room and was mildly shocked by his pale and deteriorated physical appearance.

'Well you're a sight for sore eyes', greeted Ivor, 'have you organized conjugal rights yet?'

Chris smiled in response and, unable to touch, sat opposite him at the cheap Formica table provided.

'I need to get hold of the Hahalis accounts so I can set us up for when you get out', she began.

Ivor paused thoughtfully. Could he trust this woman he thought? He would probably have to, he concluded. 'You'll need the key to the safe. That's in Sopolo's office. He comes out soon but he's had a stroke in here so he won't be much use. His daughter certainly won't help, that bitch is love-struck. I think there's a spare key to the safe taped behind his portrait in his bedroom. That's your target, but be aware: if you betray me, I'll come after you wherever you try to hide.'

She smiled reassuringly. 'I'll wait for you as long as it takes', she said, 'but I'll need help, and preferably a weapon as well'.

'Can you remember a phone number?' Ivor queried. To an assenting nod, he gave her a number and added 'that's Nicky, he's a small-time thief but he's good muscle and he has contacts. Just tell him you're working for me and he'll help.'

Farewells were perfunctory but Chris promised to keep him posted on progress. She left feeling very positive and was back in her resort by lunchtime. A call to Nicky set up a meeting for the following day.

Nicky turned out to be a young stocky Maori, broad-chested with long dark hair and deep brown eyes that seemed a little shifty to Chris and maybe too close together. He produced the goods, however. These were an older-style 9mm Browning and half a dozen rounds of ammunition for which he asked for and received $1,000 cash. Rather larger and heavier than she would have chosen for herself but beggars couldn't be choosers and she was happy with the feeling of security the pistol gave her. She briefed Nicky on her requirements, which he was content to accept, and they began their journey to Rakahanga the following day.

# CHAPTER 29

Pete, Alison, Samantha, Rebecca, baby Jeremy and nanny Emily were greeted like some long-lost tribe at their booked resort. The beach, paddling and simply lounging around occupied what was left of daylight and that whole family tribe slept soundly that night. The next morning saw much of the same for the younger people, whilst Pete headed off for his scheduled meeting with Andrew and Alison decided to touch base with her mysterious Chinese contact.

Pete greeted Andy coolly and that did not go unnoticed.

'Before you say anything, Pete, I need to explain a few things, apologize and seek your understanding', Andy began as he led them on to the verandah of a coffee house. Over coffee, he explained the relationship, or rather lack of, between he and Christine and the events that led to their marriage and what followed. Her drug habit, infidelities and inability to have children were all canvassed. He finished with is suspicions about who had set him up for his kidnapping in Rabaul and sat back looking across at Pete hopefully.

'I think I understand, Andy, although I admit to feeling enormously hurt and betrayed in the beginning. Still, it's water under the bridge now and hopefully she will stay locked up for some time yet.'

'Oh no, she escaped prison months ago', responded Andy, 'Phil Stroud the Moresby AFP officer rang to warn me. He thought she might come looking for me.'

'Forewarned is forearmed', Pete asserted and explained in very broad terms what he was doing in the Islands apart, of course, from catching up he added glibly. The brothers actually exchanged a smile for the first time in many years. 'My first port of call will be Jacob, the police skipper', Pete continued.

'I can go better than that for you,' Andy declared proudly, 'I'm on good terms with the Chief of Police and I could probably get you an interview with the Prime Minister. If you come across to Rakahanga I could add the leader of the Opposition to the list. There's a "but", though, it might have to wait a bit, I need to raise finance for the boat I'd like to buy. It's the "Blue Turtle" of not-so-happy memories and it's being auctioned tomorrow, which is really why I'm already in Rarotonga.'

'Well, that's something I might be able to fix', said Pete, thinking of Samuel Goldman, 'when do you need the funds?'

'Withing seven days of the auction', advised a very interested Andy, 'why don't you come along to the auction with me?'

They agreed to meet the following day and Pete headed for the wharf to check on the police skipper. He was warmly received and went aboard for more coffee and a chat. When the subject came around to 'Belt & Road', Jacob was more familiar with the term 'Maritime Silk Road' and had an interest in two particular aspects. One was a proposed port on Tongareva and the other the licence to fish Tuna.

'Tongareva you probably know better as Penrhyn', explained Jacob, 'it's got an airstrip which I suppose could be extended, but the main attraction is the lagoon: its enormous, must be round ninety square miles. Make a great Naval anchorage. The current issue for me is the Tuna fishing: it's licensed but only on condition the fish go back to China. We don't see any of it.'

The next day saw a small gathering overlooking the moored "Blue Turtle" awaiting the auction. Pete and Andy stood together chatting.

'So where is your lady friend Tamika', queried Pete, 'she not interested in the boat?'

'Oh yes. Tamika's my fiancée now, assuming I can arrange my divorce, but it turns out she's got a remarkable head for business. She's off in Manihiki negotiating our planned entry into the pearling business. The industry has been decimated over recent years what with cyclones and algal blooms and Tamika thinks we can re-seed the oyster beds. Long term of course, but a start would be in arranging marketing contracts. The boat would help with that and if we base it at Rakahanga it will provide for a quicker access to medical support for the islanders.'

'So, what do you think she's worth?' questioned Pete, 'the boat I mean, not Tamika.'

'I'm guessing $700k, but if it goes for anywhere near that we are out of it.'

As it transpired, bidders started dropping out much earlier at the $200k mark and as they progressively fell by the wayside Andy held the successful bid at $225k.

'My shout', yelled an ecstatic Andy, 'let's go get a drink and talk finance'.

Neither man noticed the European woman with the floppy straw hat covering her features but discreetly watching proceedings.

A phone call to Samuel Goldman revealed that he was now talking to Samuel junior, his one-time steward who, after his father's demise some months previously was now running the family's finance business. Condolences duly expressed, Pete received a firm offer of $200,000 finance for his brother at a modest 6 percent interest.

'Look, I realize you can't leave the family for too long, but why don't you and Alison join us on Rakahanga for a couple of days?' Andy suggested. 'You might enjoy some watchkeeping to help me get "Blue Turtle" across there and we could pick both Alison and Tamika up in Manihiki.'

That decided, they had a day's wait for finance and payment, with a further day for fuel and supplies. Alison booked a flight to Manihiki, cajoled the nanny into looking after all three children for a few days and they were organized. Three days later Alison met up with an excited Tamika on Manihiki and they compared notes. Tamika expounded on her business plans in the pearling arena whilst Alison spoke about their prospective, but delayed, move to a country property.

'You look particularly bright, if I may say so', commented Alison at one stage.

'I think I may be pregnant', replied Tamika cheerily, 'but Andy doesn't know and I want to save the surprise for when I'm sure.'

The following evening "Blue Turtle" arrived in port with two tired sailors aboard and they all met up for coffee and overnighted at a small but pleasant 'B&B'. Alison shared what she had heard about prospective Chinese investment in the islands. The relatively tiny ethnic Chinese population could apparently see trouble brewing. Their concern was based on the vertically integrated nature of Chinese investment: Chinese owned, staffed and supplied hotels catering for Chinese tourists. The locals could foresee resentment brewing. Pete decided that they had quite enough information to satisfy his secretive bosses and they could now simply enjoy themselves. They would all head out for Rakahanga on the morrow.

# CHAPTER 30

Christine wanted to stay ahead of the brothers she had seen together by pure chance in Rarotonga. The four-hour flight to Manihiki was no problem but she had encountered a two-day delay before the supply barge would be leaving for Rakahanga. Resigned to two nights in a small tucked-away guest house she managed to take some small pleasure in the delay. Her hired help Nicky was young and physically strong in a way she enjoyed. Accordingly, she invited him into her bed and was well satisfied with the outcome. When not satisfying her needs he was quiet and kept to himself which suited her completely.

Their barge trip to Rakahanga was uneventful and Chris exhibited all the hallmarks of one of those extremely rare tourists to the island. If anyone thought her companion a trifle unusual, they certainly were not prepared to overtly indicate so. He proved useful in negotiating the use of a 'guest hut' for a night, or possibly two, and they settled in before reconnoitering the village. The surly-looking barge skipper had said that they would be sailing the next morning but after a few crisp banknotes changed hands he suddenly realized that he and his crew needed a break and could sail the following day if necessary. Outwardly relaxed, Chris was internally focused on her objective but also contemplating her escape options. The barge was probably adequate if all went well, but Chris had her eyes on a more luxurious departure. Nicky had confidently asserted that he could handle a 75- foot cruiser by himself and that became her preferred option.

The village was neat but not extensive and the layout was fairly quickly absorbed. She passed by the police station, which was unexpectedly manned, and nodded to Nicky to take note. There were not many people wandering the main street: this was the hot and humid season and Islanders sensibly tended to take refuge in the heat of the day. She did pass one woman, somewhat better dressed than most, and they smiled at each other in a distracted sort of way. Chris would have been surprised, and possibly humoured, at the contents of an email the woman, who was the local Member Mrs Green, was carrying. This was to ask her 'with regret' to convey the condolences of the Queensland Police Force to a Mr Andrew Martyn on the unfortunate demise of his wife Christine by apparent suicide. 'Please inform him', the message read, 'that in the absence of previously contactable next-of-kin she had been buried at the Cairns Public Cemetery'.

Chris and Nicky took their evening meal early in what seemed like a communal dining hall. She was pleasantly surprised at the modest fare which included probably the freshest and tastiest Tuna she had ever enjoyed. Remaining focused on her task, however, she briefed Nicky to locate the Sopolo residence before returning to their hut.

When nightfall was as complete as it was going to become, the pair quietly headed toward the police hut. 'I need him disabled', Chris ordered, 'but try not to kill him, just make sure he can't interfere. Oh', she added 'I forgot to bring a torch, see if you can find one in there'. Saying that, she wandered away, apparently aimlessly but making sure not to go too far away from the police hut. Noise of a scuffle came from the hut but relatively subdued and then the light went out and Nicky reappeared with a torch lighting his way.

'Put that out', Chris hissed. 'Now lead the way to the Sopolo place.'

The target of their search was in fact fairly obvious, being the largest visible in the main street.

'Give me the torch', ordered Chris, 'you stay at the door and make sure I'm not interrupted'.

Going inside and flicking on the torch, the main room seemed virtually empty. Not knowing the layout, Chris took it slowly and having taken one wrong turn into a kitchen, then saw what must be the door to the bedroom. Opening the door with a slight creak she swept the torch-light around the room and settled on the bed where there were two recumbent figures.

'What the heck?' called a blinded Andy with the torch being aimed directly into his face. He started to get out of the bed, naked as he usually slept these days. He was further startled as Chris found the main light switch and turned it on.

'Well isn't this cozy', Chris chuckled evilly, 'found yourself a local slut have we husband?'

A shocked Andy moved forward only to be faced with a pistol pointing at him.

'You just stay where you are you loser', Chris directed, 'I'm here to collect what should be mine and you just need to be a good boy and stay where you are'.

Meanwhile, a sleepy Tamika was starting to get out of bed, feeling unusually vulnerable in her usually comfortable nakedness. With little option, she sat next to Andy on the edge of the bed whilst Chris was looking toward the painting of her father on the wall. Chris moved around the bed and ripped the painting off the wall and gave a small moue of relief to find a key taped to the back.

'Move or interfere with me in any way and I will take extraordinary pleasure in putting a bullet or two into that tired-looking body of yours', she announced and tore the key from its holding tape. 'Be a good little loser and his slut you two. Stay where you are and you just might survive.' She closed the bedroom door and went straight to the large old safe in the corner. The key fitted and with nerves jangling Chris knelt down and opened the heavy door. Disappointment flooded through her: she looked upon just a thick ledger, some papers that looked like bank statements and a tiny bundle of banknotes. The bedroom door then crashed open.

Andy had thrown on a pair of shorts and searched the room for a weapon of some sort. Nothing came to hand except for a solid

Maori statue which he weighed up, mentally testing its use. Throwing open the door he rushed into the main office to see his wife kneeling in front of the safe, some scattered papers and her gun on the floor beside her. He quickly, and without much thought, swung the statue at her, catching her on the shoulder and knocking her into a nearby chair. He turned away, distracted to see a large Maori entering and charging toward him. A defensive sweep of the statue caught the man's outstretched arm and they both fell to the floor in a furious exchange of fists and feet.

Tamika came out of the bedroom to the sight of the tussle on the floor, then glanced sideways to see a flustered Chris straightening herself on to one arm and raising the pistol with the other. 'Noooh!' yelled Tamika and charged at the woman. The sound of a pistol shot reverberated around the room and Tamika crumpled to the floor. There was a fleeting moment of stunned stillness in the room then a panting Alison arrived in the main doorway at a rush, closely followed by Pete. Chris was slowly rising to a kneeling position, whilst Andy had abandoned his fight and was crawling toward the prone Tamika. The pistol slowly levelled at Andy and Chris's features distorted into a fierce rage as she aimed. Those features were transformed into a look of sheer horror as a knife suddenly embedded itself in her throat. Alison's skills came to the fore yet again.

Pete walked with apparent calm into the chaos of the room as the Maori, who he later discovered to be a local called Nicky, was rising to his feet. Not one to ask unnecessary questions, Pete gave him a massive punch to the stomach and a swift uppercut to put the man unconscious on the ground. There was increasing noise from outside the main door at this stage as a small crowd of locals sought cautiously to discover the source of the gunshot.

'Someone get the policeman!' shouted Pete whilst he bent over to examine Tamika as she was being cradled in Andy's arms. He had seen enough gunshot wounds to realize immediately that this one was fatal but, leaning down anyway, he fruitlessly checked for a pulse. Tamika was dead, as was Chris who he then also confirmed had no signs of life.

It took nearly ten more minutes before an angry, confused and very sore policeman arrived at the hut and took charge of the situation.

# EPILOGUE

Peter and Alison Martyn, together with their family and nanny, eventually settled into a newly-built house on their rural property south of Sydney and began their organic skincare products business. You may perhaps be using some of their products today: it is a well-known brand appealing especially to the Asian market. Pete has continued in Naval service, although increasingly working for a government intelligence agency that shall remain nameless. His spousal security concerns were much alleviated when it was incidentally revealed that she had been temporarily employed by a sister agency called ASIO.

Andrew Martyn remained inconsolable for a very long time. He decided to remain in Rakahanga as a permanent resident and, having had his teaching credentials validated, is now a regular contributor to the education of Rakahanga's youngsters. The pearling industry has yet to achieve its historical glory days but his marketing efforts have been encouraging, as well as keeping him solvent. He recently entered into a close relationship with a fellow pearling enthusiast from Manihiki: a lady whose cheerful disposition is daily improving his demeanour. Andy is particularly well regarded in his home island for his having taken in and supported an otherwise lonely and dispirited stroke victim by the name of Michael Sopolo.

The accounts and dealings of the Hahalis Society were a quagmire that took much to unravel. Some $3.7 million sitting in the society's bank account was confiscated by the Cook Islands' government as the proceeds of crime. This action was ameliorated after pressure from the Member for Rakahanga to transfer an equivalent amount to a new Scholarship Fund to support students at Australian or New Zealand universities A number of residences in Cooktown, Australia, have been similarly acquired under Queensland law and converted for public housing use. Other elements of the society's funds proved more difficult to undo, especially an income stream that seems to have had its origins in Bitcoin. That the business acumen of the society's manager and accountant was of a very high order became apparent as the detailed accounts and accompanying notes were progressively analyzed. It became apparent early in that process that the relevant manager and accountant was one Tamika Sopolo.

A young petty criminal known locally simply as Nicky is still expected to reform his ways, having temporarily traded his occupation for that of laundry manager at Rarotonga Prison. A fellow inmate, one Ivor Slavinski, reportedly vented his anger and frustration on a guard when told of his thwarted hopes and promptly earned a further two-year extension to his confinement.

If you visit the Cook Islands, you may still see the "Blue Turtle" ferrying tourists and visiting pearl dealers between the islands, although these days she has been repainted and named "Tamika".

The benefits and less desirable impacts of Chinese investments in the islands remain under review, as does the vulnerability of the island nation to rising sea levels.

Printed in Great Britain
by Amazon